MORE TALES FROM T

FARMER JOHN'S

BLOOMERS

David C. Evans

Published in 2011 by New Generation Publishing

First Edition

Cover design by Jake Tebbit
Illustrations © Jake Tebbit 2011

For all my friends and family

Acknowledgments to Alison Hunt for her support and superb secretarial skills

List of Contents

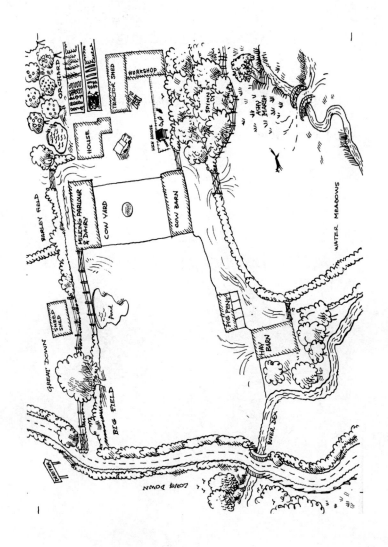

ORCHARD

TRACTOR SHED

WORKSHOP

HOUSE

HEN HOUSE

SPRING

ASH MARSH

BARLEY FIELD

MILKING PARLOUR & DAIRY

COW YARD

COW BARN

WATER MEADOWS

SHEEP SHED

Pond

PIG PENS

GREAT DOWN

HAY BARN

BIG FIELD

RIVER ISA

LONG DOWN

FARMER JOHN'S BLOOMERS

It begins to get very cold on Thistledown Farm, but

Farmer John just can't seem to keep warm...

It was a bright winter's morning on Thistledown Farm and Farmer John was having his breakfast. He tucked into his bacon and eggs.

"What lovely weather we've been having," he said to Wendy, his wife. "I think we're going to have a nice mild winter. The weatherman says that things are getting warmer - we don't seem to get winters like we used to, with all that snow and ice."

"Yes," said Wendy, "it is quite warm for the time of year. I haven't put a pullover on yet, and it's nearly December."

Farmer John smiled. "If it keeps on like this," he said, "I'm going to have to put my shorts on."

Wendy laughed. "What! And show off those pale spindly legs? No, thank you."

"But I've got nice legs," said Farmer John.

"They're all hairy and horrible," said Wendy, "and you've got knobbly knees too."

"Rubbish," said Farmer John, "my legs are very shapely!" He put on his cap and went out in a huff.

Daisy the dairy cow was standing in the yard after milking. "Moo!" she said. "Morning John, how are you today?"

"I'm fed up," said Farmer John. "Wendy's being very rude about my legs."

Daisy laughed. "What's wrong with them?" she said.

"Wendy thinks they're all pale and thin and knobbly and hairy and horrible," said Farmer John.

"Oh, you don't want to worry about what people think of your legs," said Daisy. "Look at mine, they're all hairy and I've got four of them. You've only got two - that gives you half as much to worry about."

"Maybe," said Farmer John.

"You want to show them off," said Daisy. "Why not put some shorts on? The weather's nice; you might get a suntan."

"Good idea," said Farmer John. "I think I might just do that." He rushed back to the farmhouse and dashed upstairs. He came down a few minutes later wearing a pair of baggy khaki shorts.

Wendy laughed when she saw him. "Gracious," she said, "you're not going out looking like that, are you?"

"I am," said Farmer John. "You said my legs looked pale, so I'm going to get a suntan."

He put on his boots and went out. Mavis the ewe was nibbling some hay when he reached the sheep shed. "Baa," she said. "What's happened to your trousers, John, have they shrunk in the wash?"

"No," said Farmer John crossly. "I'm wearing my shorts. It's so warm for the time of year I thought I'd get a suntan."

Mavis laughed. "Your legs are too pale," she said, "but they'll probably get very brown if you wear shorts around the farm all the time - they'll get all mucky."

Farmer John frowned. "Maybe," he said. "I'll have to be careful." He gave Mavis some sheep nuts and pushed off to see the pigs.

Suzie the sow was scratching herself on the pig-pen wall. "Morning, John," she said. "What's wrong with your legs? There's something growing on them."

Farmer John looked down. "It's my leg hair," he said. "It's quite natural, they're meant to be like that."

Suzie laughed. "If you say so," she said, "but isn't it the wrong time of year to be wearing shorts?"

"Not really," said Farmer John. "You can wear shorts any time as long as the weather's nice." He gave Suzie her food and trudged off.

The sky started to turn grey and an icy wind began to blow. Farmer John began to feel a little cold. The wind whipped around his legs and little goose bumps started to appear. He shivered; he only had a T shirt on. "Bother," he said, "where's the sun gone? My legs aren't going to get much of a tan in this weather." He tried to ignore the

9

weather but it got colder and colder and colder until he was shivering so much that his teeth began to chatter.

Little blocks of ice formed around his knees, and his fingers started to turn blue. His ears stung in the wind and a tiny icicle hung from the end of his nose. He rubbed his hands together to keep them warm, but it didn't make any difference. "I've had enough of this," he said. "I'm going to put something on." He marched back to the farmhouse, his wellies flapping against his spindly little legs.

When he came down from his bedroom a little while later he was wearing a pair of warm gloves, two pairs of socks, three pullovers, four big winter coats and five woolly hats pulled down over his ears.

"There," he said, "that should do it." He pulled on his wellies and went out into the yard. He marched across to the dairy, but halfway there he slipped on a nasty patch of slippery black ice and landed –"OUCH!" - on his bottom. "Rats!" he said as he got up. "So much for a nice mild winter."

He went into the dairy. All the pipes were frozen up. He tried to start Tommy his tractor but his engine was too cold. "Bother this," he said. "It's freezing out here! I'm going back inside in the warm."

Wendy was in the sitting room when he got in. She was standing by the fire. "Come in, John," she said. "You must be cold."

"I am, actually," said Farmer John. "It's funny but I've got all these clothes on, and I'm absolutely freezing."

"Oh," said Wendy, "that's strange. I wonder why that is?"

"I don't know," said Farmer John. He sat and shivered on the settee.

"Can I have a hot water bottle?" he asked eventually.

"Goodness," said Wendy, "you *are* cold, aren't you!" She filled a hot water bottle and gave it to him. Farmer John hugged it. His nose was blue and his teeth were chattering.

"I don't know why you're so freezing," said Wendy. "You've got five woolly hats, four big coats, three pullovers, two pairs of socks and a pair of warm gloves on."

Farmer John sat up. "But I haven't got any knickers on!" he said.

Wendy laughed. "Really! Why's that?"

"Well, when I changed I couldn't find any," said Farmer John. "All my underpants have gone missing."

"Oh," said Wendy, "so that's why you're so cold! You'd better come with me - I've got something to show you." Wendy put on her boots and led Farmer John over to see his animals. Daisy the dairy cow, Suzie the sow and Mavis the ewe all had pairs of brightly patterned underpants over their ears.

"I think I owe you an explanation," said Wendy. "All your animals had such cold ears that I gave them your knickers to keep them warm."

Farmer John laughed. "Of course - what a good idea - but what about me...how am *I* going to keep warm?"

"You can borrow a pair of my bloomers," said Wendy, "until the weather gets better."

"Oh...OK," said Farmer John. "As long as you don't tell anyone!"

So Farmer John wore Wendy's bloomers and the animals wore Farmer John's knickers and everyone on Thistledown Farm kept very warm indeed.

Farmer John was a bit relieved when the weather changed and he got his underwear back. "Your bloomers are all right, Wendy," he said, "but I think they're a bit too frilly for me."

Wendy laughed. "I thought you looked very nice in them," she said. "Perhaps I should buy you some for your birthday."

"No fear," said Farmer John. "I think they look much better on you! And they gave each other a huge hug.

Farmer John decides to make butter; but it isn't long

before he has more than he knows what to do with!

It was springtime at Thistledown Farm, and Farmer John was up and about milking his cows.

"What a lot of milk I've got this morning," he said as he put the clusters on the cows' udders. "It must be all that fresh spring grass - you cows are certainly milking well."

"MOO!" said Daisy, "I'm bursting. Hurry up. I don't think I can hold on much longer!"

Farmer John put the teat cups on Daisy's teats. "There you are," he said. "How much have you got for me this morning?"

"Ooh, about five gallons," said Daisy, "and I shouldn't be surprised if I don't have more tomorrow. That grass is really lush - it's full of goodness, you know."

Farmer John rubbed his hands together. "Excellent," he said. "I like to have a lot of milk to send to the dairy, because then I get more money."

He finished milking Daisy and let her out of the parlour. "There," he said, "that was the last cow. Let's go over and see how much milk I've got in the tank." He toddled across to the tank room but before he could open the door a huge puddle of milk appeared, spilling out into the yard. "Oh my goodness!" cried Farmer John. "The tank has overflowed!" He slid open the door and peered inside. The place was awash with milk and the tank was brimful.

"Oh no," groaned Farmer John. "I've got too much milk. What am I going to do with it all?"

Just then the milk lorry arrived. "Morning, John," said the driver. "What's up? It looks like you've had an accident."

"My cows are milking so well," said Farmer John, "that I can't fit it all into the tank."

The driver chuckled. "No use crying over spilt milk, John," he said. "You'll have to get another tank to put it in."

"But I can't afford it," said Farmer John. "I've got no money to spare."

"Oh dear," said the driver. "Perhaps you'll have to drink it yourself to use it all up."

"Very funny," said Farmer John. "I'd have to drink milk all day long to do that!"

"Oh well," said the driver, "you'll think of something." He uncoiled a length of pipe, pumped the milk out of the tank into the lorry, and drove off.

Farmer John hosed out the tank and went into the house for his breakfast. Wendy, his wife, was in the kitchen. "Morning, John," she called cheerily. "How was the milking?"

"All right," said Farmer John, "but I've got a problem. I've got too much milk and I can't think what to do with it all."

"Oh dear," said Wendy. "Perhaps we could make some cheese or yoghurt or cream with it...I know, let's turn it into butter!"

"What a good idea," said Farmer John. "That's a good way to store unwanted milk."

So that evening, at milking time, Wendy collected buckets and buckets of milk from the tank and brought them into the kitchen. She put the milk through a separator to skim off the cream, and Farmer John fed the skimmed milk to the pigs. Wendy turned the cream in a butter-maker. It was hard work and Wendy's arm ached as she turned the handle. Soon though, after lots of effort, the cream began to go solid and thump around inside the barrel. Wendy opened the lid and removed a huge lump of butter. She made it into pats and wrapped them in greaseproof paper. She was ready to sit down when she had finished.

Farmer John was very pleased when he came in from milking. There was a huge pile of butter on the kitchen table. "Goodness," he said to Wendy. "You *have* made a lot. Where are you going to put it all?"

"Oh, it can go in the fridge," said Wendy. So they packed the butter into the fridge. It filled up every shelf.

"There," said Farmer John. "Now, what's for dinner?"

"Dinner?" said Wendy. "I haven't had time to cook dinner. You'll have to make something yourself - I'm too tired."

"WHAT!" cried Farmer John. "But I'm starving!"

"Too bad," said Wendy. "You can open a tin of beans. I'm off to bed!" And she went upstairs.

"Oh dear," thought Farmer John. "This butter-making lark is hard work. Poor Wendy!" And he sat and munched his beans on toast.

Next morning Wendy made butter again, and did so again in the evening. She made butter the next day and the day after that and the day after that until she had so much butter she had nowhere left to put it all. She'd filled up the fridge and the cupboards and the larder. She'd filled up the kitchen and the cold store and the bathroom. She'd filled up the woodshed and the workshop and the dairy, and she was tired and cross! "What are we going to do with all this butter?" she complained.

"I don't know," said Farmer John. "Perhaps we ought to start eating it?"

So Farmer John and Wendy started eating the butter. They had butter on their toast and butter on their potatoes. They had butter on their parsnips, butter on their beans, and butter on their carrots. They had butter on their biscuits and butter on their cake. They had butter on their pancakes and

Wendy made lots of buttery scones and sauces, but still they had lots of butter left over. Farmer John put butter on the bird table for the birds. He fed butter to his pigs and he tried melted butter instead of diesel for Tommy, his tractor, but Tommy didn't like it very much. It clogged up his fuel pipes!

Farmer John and Wendy were soon sick of eating so much butter and so were the pigs and the birds. "What can we do now?" said Wendy. "We've still got heaps of it left."

"I know," said Farmer John. "I'll take it all up to the end of the lane. The dustmen can take it away." So Farmer John loaded up his trailer and dumped a great pile at the end of the lane by the road. He was pleased to get rid of it!

But next morning, when the dustmen came, they left the butter mountain behind. It was far too sticky to put in their dustcart - it would have gummed up the works - and when Farmer John went to the end of the lane later that day, he groaned in despair. "However am I going to get rid of all this butter?" he moaned.

Just then a car passed by, braked suddenly, and reversed back to where Farmer John was standing. Four odd-looking people got out and started peering at the pile of half-melted butter. "How amazing," said one, "to find such a perfect installation out in the middle of nowhere like this!" The others nodded their heads furiously.

They turned to Farmer John. "Is this *your* work?" said a thin woman in black. "And what is your inspiration for the piece? To which school of art do you belong and what statement are you trying to make? It is obviously a witty piece – am I right?"

Farmer John thought furiously. "Well, I'm a conceptual artist and I use butter in all my work, as it is a medium well suited to sculpture. In this particular piece I'm poking fun at table manners and how we are taught not to play with our food. I'm making a serious statement about human behaviour by making such a large exhibit!"

All the artists opened their mouths in astonishment. "But of course!" they cried. "How could we have missed it? Such a subtle statement, yet so obvious. How much do you want for it?"

Farmer John racked his brains. "Well, I wasn't going to sell it you see, puts me in a very difficult position. Hmm. Have to think about it."

"How about a thousand pounds?" said the artist with a cloak and Fedora hat. "I simply must have it in my gallery. Will you take cash?"

Farmer John couldn't believe his ears. A thousand pounds for a load of old rancid butter. It was too good to be true. He'd better get the money quick, before they changed their minds!

Wendy was very curious when Farmer John came back from the end of the lane, counting his notes. "Why are you looking so happy?" she asked.

"Because I've just become a successful artist," he said, and he gave her the thousand pounds. "You didn't know, did you, dear, that I created masterpieces of genius? In years to come, people will flock from all over the world to stare at my work and say "Now *that* is a 'John Stubblefield!'"

FARMER JOHN'S WISH

Farmer John's neighbour Brian starts a new enterprise;

but it takes off sooner than he expects!

It was a wet and windy afternoon on Thistledown Farm, and Farmer John was looking over the hedge. The rain trickled down his red face and dripped from the end of his nose. "What a miserable day," he thought. "Farming's such a hard life...there must be easier ways to make a living!"

The sheep huddled together in a corner of the field with their backs to the wind. Farmer John tried to count them but kept losing his place.

"One two, one two three, one two...Oh dear," he thought. "Perhaps I should count their legs and divide by four." He tried that but had to give up; the sheep were too close together. "Bother," he said to himself. "Never mind; it looks like they're all there. I think I'll just go home for a cup of tea." He looked over the hedge again, into his neighbour's field. He smiled to himself. "Brian's got more weeds than I have," he said. "He's got lots of thistles and docks. I'll have to pull his leg about that," and he toddled back to the farmhouse for some tea.

Next door in Brian's field a lorry came through the gate, and workmen got out. They unloaded some huge white poles and started putting them together with nuts and bolts, and a crane lifted them into the air. Soon there were six tall poles sticking up out of the ground like huge mushroom stalks. Each pole had three long white blades attached to the top, and they began to go round and round in the wind. They made a strange wailing noise and the sheep were quite alarmed. "BAAAH!" they cried. "What's thaaat!" They ran across the field and through the hedge into Farmer John's cornfield next door. They began to nibble the young corn plants!

Meanwhile, back at the farmhouse, Farmer John sat in the kitchen. "Brian's got more weeds than me," he said to Wendy, his wife. "I was just looking, and he's got heaps of docks and thistles. I thought I had more thistles than anyone else around here - perhaps I'm doing something right for a change!"

Wendy laughed. "The reason he's got thistles and docks next door is that they've probably come from you," she said. "Thistledown blows on the wind, you know."

"Oh dear," said Farmer John. "Do you really think so?"

"Don't worry," said Wendy. "He can't prove that they came from you - you can always say that you got your thistles from him!"

Farmer John laughed. "That's a good idea," he said. "What a clever wife I've got; you know, sometimes I think you'd do a better job of running the farm than me."

Wendy smiled. "Perhaps you're right," she said, "but I've got quite enough to do without all the farm work as well. You're not such a bad farmer - it's not your fault things go wrong sometimes."

"You say the kindest things," said Farmer John, "but Brian next door's always doing better than me. Nothing ever goes wrong on his farm."

"But we have more fun," said Wendy. "Life on Thistledown Farm is never dull."

Farmer John smiled. "I'm glad," he said, "but sometimes I wish something would go wrong on Brian's farm, just for once, to make me feel better!"

He got up and went to the window. "When's it going to stop raining?" he complained. "I'm fed up with getting wet all the time...what the ...!" He peered through the misty glass. "My sheep are in the cornfield!" he cried. "Now that's all I need!" He rushed to the door, jumped into his boots, threw his coat and cap on and dashed out into the yard.

He hurried across the fields, opened the gate into the corn and chased his sheep out, waving his stick around in the air. "Blimmin' animals," he puffed to himself. "One minute they're perfectly happy, and the next they're up to their old tricks." He shut the gate and stopped to get his breath back. He paused and cocked his head. "What's that noise?" he said. From across the field came an eerie sound …"WOOOEEEOOOEEEOOO…"

"Sounds like some kind of ghost," thought Farmer John. He was a little worried; he was a bit afraid of ghosts! "Surely ghosts don't go haunting in the daytime?" he said. He marched across the field and peeped over the hedge.

"Heavens above! What on earth has Brian got in his field?" thought Farmer John. "They must be fast growing; they weren't there when I was here earlier. They don't look like any weeds I've seen before…I wonder what they could be?"

Just then, up popped Brian on the other side of the hedge. "Hello John," he said. "I knew you'd be along sooner or later - what do you think of my new wind farm?"

"Wind farm?" said Farmer John. "How can you farm the wind? You can't even see it!"

Brian laughed. "It's called 'renewable energy,' he said. "My windmills use the power of the wind to make electricity. I keep some for myself and all the rest I can sell to other people; it's a real money spinner!"

"Really!" said Farmer John excitedly. "And what do you have to do?"

"Nothing," said Brian. "I don't have to feed them or milk them twice a day...it's all so easy, I don't know why I haven't done it before."

"Hmm," said Farmer John, scratching his chin. "There must be a catch somewhere."

"No catch," said Brian, "any idiot can do it!"

"Is that so?" said Farmer John, interested.

"Yes," said Brian. "I'm going to sell all my animals and retire. I'll never have to work again!"

But just then there was an almighty gust of wind, and Brian's hat flew off. The wind howled and the windmills creaked and groaned in the gale. Farmer John watched Brian chase after his hat, bowling across the field. All of a sudden the ground gave a tremendous shudder and Farmer John looked on as the windmills heaved themselves up into the air and took off, carrying the field and Brian with them!

"HELP!" Brian clung tight to a windmill as the wind farm blew away in the storm like a vast helicopter.

"Oh dear," thought Farmer John. "I wonder where *he'll* end up!" He peered into the gaping hole left by the field. He remembered his wish that something would go wrong on

Brian's farm, and felt a little bit guilty. "Be careful what you wish for," he thought. "You may get what you want!"

He trudged back to the farmhouse, bent double against the wind. He took off his boots and sat and turned on the telly. It was the news. There was a picture of Brian and his wind farm perched on top of the highest mountain in Scotland!

Farmer John chuckled to himself. "I hope Brian gets back in time to milk his cows," he said. "Perhaps my way of farming's not such a hard life after all. Wind farming seems much more risky to me!"

Just then Wendy came in. "Wind farming?" she said. "Who's been wind farming?"

Farmer John laughed. "Oh, only Brian next door," he said with a huge grin on his face. "According to him, any idiot can do it!" And he rubbed his hands together with glee!

FARMER JOHN'S PURCHASE

Farmer John buys a cow at market, but Daffodil

doesn't get on very well with the rest of the herd...

One morning, Farmer John was buttering his toast at breakfast when he had an idea. "I know what," he said to Wendy, his wife. "I feel like going to market today, just to see what the prices are like."

"OK," said Wendy, "but be careful you don't buy anything you don't want to."

"Don't worry," said Farmer John. "I know what I'm doing. I've been to market more times than you've had hot dinners!"

Wendy laughed. "That's quite a few," she said, "but I know you - you're bound to do something silly."

"Rubbish," said Farmer John. "I'm the most sensible farmer in the county - I never do anything wrong."

"Hmm!" thought Wendy.

Farmer John finished his coffee and went to feed his animals. When he had done that he jumped into Lawrence the Landrover and set off for Dexeter Market.

There were lots of people about when he arrived. The car park was nearly full and he had to drive around looking for a parking space. Finally he found one and, leaving Lawrence to talk to the car next door, he marched off to see the sheep being sold.

The auctioneer was busy taking bids as he pushed his way to the front. "At fifty, fifty, fifty, fifty-two, fifty-four, fifty-six," he went. Farmers in flat caps were bidding keenly for pens of ewes. "Those sheep look smart," thought Farmer John, "and a good price too. Fifty-six pounds...I must remember that. I wonder what the pigs are making?"

He went over to the pig pens. There weren't many farmers there. "Not much interest here," he thought. "I expect those pigs will be cheap with no one to buy them. What a pity that I don't need any at the moment. My pens are all full up. Now, I wonder what the dairy cows are fetching."

He pushed his way through the crowd to the front of the ring. Black and white dairy cows were walking around hoping for someone to buy them. "At 400, 400," sang the auctioneer. Farmer John scratched his nose; it was a little itchy. "At 450, 450," went the auctioneer. Farmer John tugged at his ear. "500, 500." Farmer John rubbed his eye, he was a little tired. "At 550, 550," said the auctioneer. Farmer John sneezed. "SOLD TO FARMER JOHN," shouted the auctioneer, "for 600 guineas …"

"WHAT!" Farmer John called to the auctioneer. "But I wasn't bidding!" All the other farmers laughed.

"It looked like you were bidding to me," said the auctioneer. "You've got yourself a new cow, John."

"Oh," said Farmer John. "What am I going to do with her?"

"Take her home," said the other farmers. "She looks like a good milker."

Farmer John had to pay up. "It's a good job I've got the money," he grumbled. "I wasn't expecting to come home with anything today. Oh well!" He loaded his new cow into Lawrence's stock trailer.

Lawrence chuckled. "It's a good job I bought the trailer with me, John - I know what you're like."

Farmer John drove home. When he got back, Wendy was waiting for him. "How did it go, John?" she asked.

"I bought a cow by mistake," he said.

Wendy burst out laughing. "I knew you'd do something daft," she said. "What are you going to do now?"

"Put her with the rest of the cows," said Farmer John. "She can join the herd; she looks like she'd milk well."

Farmer John's new cow introduced herself to the others. "I'm Daffodil," she said, "and you're Daisy, I presume. How do you do? I come from a long line of superior pedigree animals. I can trace my ancestry back many, many years."

"Really," said Daisy. "That's nice."

"I have breeding," said Daffodil. "My father was the best bull in the whole county, and always won first prize at the county show."

Daisy was getting a bit fed up with Daffodil's boasting. "My milk yields," continued Daffodil, "are the highest since records began, and my daughters have all gone on to become champion animals."

All the cows began to grumble. "What a stuck up cow," they said. "She thinks she's better than us." Daffodil went and lay down in a corner by herself. "I'm not mixing with that riff-raff," she said. "They're all beneath me. What sort of a dairy farm is this?"

Farmer John came along. "Now then Daffodil," he said, "how are you getting on - making lots of new friends, are we?"

Daffodil snorted. "All your cows are common," she said. "I can't talk to *them* - and by the way, this straw is too prickly. I need some soft barley straw to lie down in, and I need my food chopped and brought to me, and I wish to be milked last in the morning. I need my beauty sleep, you know."

Farmer John was a little taken aback. "Really," he said, "there's nothing wrong with *my* cows. I'll have you know that Daisy always wins first prize at the dairy competition every year."

"Well, *she* may be all right," said Daffodil, "but the others ..." Farmer John was a bit cross.

"Now look here, Daffodil," he said, "if you don't like it here I can always take you back to market."

"Oh, please," said Daffodil. "I can't bear to have such awful company!"

So next morning Farmer John drove Daffodil back to market, but when she went into the ring no-one wanted to buy her. She was left all on her own in a pen.

"I can't understand it," said Farmer John. "Why has nobody been bidding?"

"Don't you know, John?" said the other farmers. "Everyone knows that cow - she's so stuck up she's been to every farm in the district and wherever she goes, she complains. Nobody wants *her* - you'll have to take her back."

"Oh dear," said Farmer John. "What am I going to do? She doesn't get on with my cows. Oh well, we'll have to go back, I suppose." He loaded Daffodil up and drove home in silence.

Daffodil was very upset that nobody wanted her. All the other cows laughed. "It's not surprising with your attitude," they said. "In this life you have to make friends where you can."

Daffodil went off and thought for a while. "Perhaps I am a little too fussy," she said. "We're all cows after all, and it doesn't do to go making enemies. Maybe if I was a little friendlier things might get better."

The cows felt a bit sorry for Daffodil, and she soon began to make a few friends and fit in and get on. She became less selfish and snobby and ate with the rest of the herd at mealtimes. Farmer John was pleased.

"That Daffodil's getting on really well now," he said to Wendy. "It just goes to show that with a little effort we can all be friends."

Daffodil still thinks she is a bit different but everyone is different in their own way, as Daffodil has learned.

FARMER JOHN'S DEAL

Farmer John tries to do a deal with his neighbour, but ends up with the short end of the bargain!

It was a rainy afternoon on Thistledown Farm and Farmer John was sitting in his office, sipping a cup of tea and doing sums on his calculator. Wendy his wife came in. "What are you up to, John?" she asked.

"I'm sorting out my business," said Farmer John. "Things are not going well. I may have to swap some of my animals."

"Oh dear," said Wendy. "That doesn't sound too good."

"Don't worry, my dear," said Farmer John. "I'm a good businessman; I'm clever at doing a deal."

"Maybe," said Wendy, "but you be careful. I know what you're like. You'd probably swap a cow for a chicken and think you got a bargain."

"Huh," said Farmer John, "don't be ridiculous. I'd never do anything as silly as that."

"Hmm," said Wendy. "I'm not so sure. Perhaps you ought to leave it to me."

"No fear," said Farmer John. "I'm in charge here. Now go away and let me get on with it."

"OK," said Wendy, "but I bet you do something daft," and she went out and banged the door.

Farmer John sat and prodded the buttons on his calculator. "I reckon," he said to himself, "that I need one less cow, two more sheep and three more pigs. Hmm," and he scratched his chin. "I know, I'll ring up Brian my neighbour. He might be able to help." He picked up the phone and dialled a number.

"Hello neighbour," said Farmer John. "Can you come over? I think I have a deal which might interest you."

"OK," said Brian. "I'll be five minutes," and he put the phone down.

Farmer John was in the yard when Brian drove in on his tractor. "Hello, John," he said. "What's this deal you're on about?"

Farmer John smiled. "Well," he said, "I've got a cow to swap. Daisy's her name. She's a lovely milker but I can't afford to keep her. Can I swap her for two sheep and three pigs?"

"Hmm," said Brian, "two sheep and three pigs eh? That sounds rather a lot. What about one sheep and two pigs?"

Farmer John scratched his head. "I don't know," he said.

"Tell you what I'll do," said Brian. "I'll give you two pigs and a hen." Farmer John looked puzzled. "Maybe," he said.

"Just for you," said Brian, "I'll give you no pigs and two hens."

"Goodness," said Farmer John. "That sounds generous."

"Even better," said Brian, "I'll let you have just one hen."

"Done," said Farmer John.

"You have been!" said Brian. "Can I take Daisy now?"

"Of course," said Farmer John.

"And here's the hen," said Brian, and he reached into his tractor cab and brought out a little speckled chicken.

Farmer John looked pleased. "What a lovely bird," he said. "Does it lay any eggs?"

"None at all," said Brian. "That's why I've swapped it - cheerio!' He drove off with Daisy in his stock trailer.

Farmer John picked up the hen and toddled across the yard to the chicken coop. He popped the bird inside. "There you are," he said, "you'll be quite happy in there. Make yourself at home," and he shut the door.

When Farmer John came in for lunch, Wendy was waiting for him. "Well?" she said. "Did you get what you wanted?"

"Oh yes," said Farmer John. "I got a bargain."

"Thank goodness for that," said Wendy. "I was a bit worried."

"I swapped Daisy for a chicken," said Farmer John.

"WHAT!" Wendy opened and shut her mouth. "JOHN STUBBLEFIELD, you stupid man - and I thought I was joking! You really are the most hopeless farmer! A cow for a chicken - what *were* you thinking of?"

"But it's a very nice chicken," said Farmer John.

"It had better be," said Wendy. "Don't tell me - it lays golden eggs?"

"Er, it doesn't lay any eggs at all actually," said Farmer John. "That's why Brian wanted to swap it."

"TCHAH!" said Wendy. "And you call yourself a good businessman. Really, sometimes I wonder."

Farmer John went and hid in his office. Wendy was very cross with him. "Oh dear," he thought, "perhaps it wasn't a very good deal after all. It is a very tiny chicken and I didn't get the sheep and pigs I wanted. Never mind; maybe it isn't as bad as it seems." He put his cap over his eyes and went to sleep.

Wendy was very quiet at dinner time that day and when Farmer John and Wendy went to bed she wasn't speaking to him. "Deary me," thought Farmer John, "that neighbour of mine has a lot to answer for. I think I'll go over and see him tomorrow and see if I can get Daisy back," and he turned over and switched off the light.

When he woke up the next morning the sun was streaming through the curtains. Wendy was up and about, but she hadn't brought him a cup of tea. "She's still upset with me," thought Farmer John. "I'm going to see that neighbour of mine right now - he'd better give me back my cow!" He dressed in a hurry and hopped into Lawrence the Landrover.

He drove into Brian's yard. Brian was milking his cows. "Hello, John," he said. "You were right about Daisy - she's a very good milker. She's given lots of milk this morning, look!" He showed Farmer John a full churn.

"That's what I wanted to see you about," said Farmer John. "I want to swap Daisy back for that chicken."

"Ha!" laughed Brian. "We did a deal - you can't go back on it now."

"But Wendy's very upset," said Farmer John. "She's not speaking to me."

"That's not my problem," said Brian. "You should have thought of that yesterday when we were bargaining."

"Oh well," said Farmer John. "No harm in asking," and he drove off home.

When he got back to the yard he was met by Wendy coming back from the chicken run. "John," she cried. "You'll never guess what! Your chicken has just laid a dozen eggs - look." And she showed Farmer John a big tray full.

"Gosh!" said Farmer John, "She must like it here. Brian said she didn't lay any eggs."

"I know," said Wendy. "If she keeps on like this we'll have heaps to sell."

Just then, who should come trotting down the lane, but Daisy! "Moo," she said. "I don't like it next door, I'm homesick. I want to come back and live on Thistledown Farm again."

Farmer John was overjoyed. "Welcome home, Daisy," he said. "I'm glad to have you back."

It wasn't long before Brian came down the lane from next door. "My cow's run off," he said. "Have you seen her?"

"Yes," said Farmer John, "she's come back to live with me because she's homesick. You can't keep her, I'm afraid."

"In that case," said Brian, "I want my chicken back."

"I'm sorry," said Farmer John, "but we did a deal, remember?"

"But now I'm left with nothing," complained Brian.

"OK," said Farmer John. "You can have your chicken back, but only if you give me the pigs and sheep that I wanted."

Brian shrugged his shoulders. "You win," he said. So Brian gave Farmer John his sheep and pigs and Farmer John let Brian have his chicken. She was sorry to leave because she had got to like being on Thistledown Farm, but she soon got used to being with Brian again and laid him a few eggs, now and then - but only when she felt like it!

Wendy was very pleased with Farmer John. "You got your sheep and pigs and you managed to keep Daisy too," she said. "Now that's what I call a good deal."

"Yes," said Farmer John. "I've been doing my sums again and I think I can keep Daisy on now."

"You're quite a good businessman after all," said Wendy. "I take back everything I said."

"Thank you," said Farmer John. "And you're quite a good wife too."

"John Stubblefield, you say the nicest things," said Wendy, and they gave each other a huge hug.

FARMER JOHN'S SAUSAGE

Farmer John decides to make sausages, but things don't quite go according to plan …

It was a bright morning on Thistledown Farm and Farmer John was having his breakfast. "These are rather nice sausages, my dear," he said to Wendy his wife. "Where do they come from?"

"They're from the butchers in Dexeter," said Wendy. "They've got pork and herbs and spices and red wine and beer and cider in them."

"Goodness," said Farmer John. "I'd better not have too many - I might get tipsy."

Wendy laughed. "I don't think you can get tipsy by eating sausages," she said, "but perhaps you shouldn't have too many...you'll get fat!"

"Rubbish," said Farmer John. "Hardworking farmers need feeding just like their animals," and he helped himself to six more sausages. He munched them slowly, enjoying their flavour. "I've had an idea," he said to Wendy, "why don't *I* make some sausages? I'm sure I could make some even tastier ones. My grandma had a secret recipe she used to make super sausages, I remember, when I was a boy."

Wendy laughed. "Good idea," she said, "it might save us a bit of money. Why don't you try it?"

So when he had finished breakfast, Farmer John jumped into Lawrence the Landrover and dashed into town. He came back a little while later with a rather strange looking contraption.

"Heavens," said Wendy when she saw him. "What on earth is that?"

"It's my sausage making machine," said Farmer John. "I can't wait to try it out. Have you got any pork?" Wendy gave him a big bag of pork mince and Farmer John collected all the secret ingredients for his grandma's recipe from the kitchen. He picked up some salt and some sugar. He found some pepper and some hot chilli powder. He got some English mustard, some horseradish sauce, some redcurrant jelly and some sprigs of mint from the garden. Finally he picked up a bottle of Worcestershire sauce, a clove of garlic, and last but not least a bottle of beer.

"Right," he said. "Now I'm ready." He went into his workshop and closed the door. He plugged the sausage making machine in and began feeding the ingredients into it. The sausages started to come out, but they came out very slowly. Farmer John was a bit impatient. "Come on, come on," he said, as he waited for each sausage to appear. "This is no good," he said, and he turned a dial on the machine. Things began to speed up. Strings of sausages began to shoot out of the machine. Farmer John had a bit of trouble keeping up. The sausages wrapped themselves around his legs and he fell over - "OOF!" - onto the floor.

"STOP, STOP!" he yelled, but the machine didn't listen. It got faster and faster and faster, until Farmer John was covered by a heap of sausages on the floor. He tried to get up, but he couldn't move!

"Help! Help!" he cried. Finally, the machine ran out of ingredients and came to a stop. Farmer John wriggled and wriggled but he couldn't get free of his sausages - they had tied him up like a rope. "Rats," he said. "What am I going to do!" Eventually, after a lot of effort, he managed to stand up. He couldn't move his arms; he had coils and coils of sausages wrapped around him like a huge snake. He hopped to the door.

"Let me out! Let me out!" he shouted. Wendy heard him and came running. She slid open the door.

"Heavens, John," she said. "What *have* you been doing?"

"I've been attacked by my sausages," said Farmer John. "They're trying to eat me!"

"Goodness," said Wendy, "I thought you were supposed to eat *them*." She grabbed hold of the end of the sausages and gave a pull. Farmer John span around as she pulled, and he got quite giddy. Wendy wound the sausages up in a bundle. "There," she said. "I don't think these sausages can be that dangerous, they seem quite well behaved to me. I didn't think you were going to make so many. What are we going to do with them all?"

Farmer John thought. "I know!" he said. "The weather's nice - we can have a barbecue."

"What a good idea!" said Wendy. "Barbecued sausages taste so nice." So Farmer John began to make a barbecue. He got an old oil drum and cut it in half. He got some wood and put it in the drum and put some wire mesh across the top. Then he piled all the sausages on the mesh.

"There," he said, "we'll soon get those sausages cooking." He found some matches and tried to light the fire, but the wind kept blowing the matches out. "Bother," he said. "We won't have anything to eat at this rate. I know - I'll get some diesel." He rushed off to the tractor shed and came back with a big can.

He splosed the diesel over the wood. "Right," he said, "now we can start cooking." He lit a match. WOOF! A huge flame shot up into the air and singed his eyebrows. "Ouch!" he cried - his face had turned black with soot. The barbecue was roaring, and tall flames shot up to the sky. The heat was fierce and little smuts got in Farmer John's eyes.

Suddenly Farmer John remembered.

"MY SAUSAGES!" he cried, and dashed forward and tried to rescue them but was beaten back by the flames. He tried again and nearly got there but he burnt his fingers - "OUCH, OUCH, OUCH!" Then he realised that his wellies were melting! His feet were very hot inside his boots as he hopped and skipped around. "I'd better get some help," he thought, and he rushed down to the house and rang up the fire brigade.

Stan the Fireman came racing into the yard on his big red fire engine. He uncoiled a hose and water gushed out. Farmer John was in the way. He got soaked. "Not me, you fool," he shouted, "I'm not on fire! Put out the barbecue!" Stan the Fireman turned his hose on the barbecue. There was a big hissing noise and the flames began to go down. Soon the fire was put out.

Stan the Fireman looked at the barbecue. There was a pile of black cinders where Farmer John's sausages had been. "I think your sausages are a bit overcooked," said Stan to Farmer John. He picked one up and examined it.

Farmer John groaned. "My lovely sausages," he moaned. "I made them myself you know - they were my grandma's special recipe."

"Oh dear," said Stan.

"Never mind," said Farmer John. "I'll make some more another day." Just then there was a clap of thunder and a flash of lightning. Rain came bucketing down and Farmer John and Stan raced into the house for shelter.

Wendy was in the kitchen making some tea. "I'm afraid I burnt the sausages, dear," said Farmer John. "I don't think I'm very good at barbecuing."

"Never mind," said Wendy, "have a ham sandwich instead," and she gave them both a plateful.

The next day, Farmer John tried his sausage machine out again. He put all the ingredients in and flipped a switch, but this time something else went wrong. Instead of lots of little sausages coming out, he got one huge sausage as big as a marrow. "Bless my soul!" said Farmer John. "That must be a record breaker."

A man came to weigh and measure the sausage and it was declared the biggest sausage in the world. Farmer John was quite proud of owning the champion sausage, and he put it in a case on his mantelpiece.

But it didn't last for very long. He got a bit peckish one night and fried it. It was delicious. "My grandma's recipe's very good," said Farmer John to Wendy, "but I think it needs just a little bit more salt and pepper."

FARMER JOHN'S OLYMPICS

Farmer John and his neighbour Brian decide to hold a contest to see whose animals are best!

One evening Farmer John was sitting on his sofa, watching telly with Brian his neighbour. They had finished work and were sharing a can of cider.

"I'm bored," said Farmer John. "Nothing's happened round here for ages."

"You're right," said Brian. "We need to do something."

Just then there was a fanfare of trumpets, and a runner holding a torch of flames appeared on the TV. The man ran up some steps and lit a huge beacon, surrounded by a stadium full of thousands of spectators.

"It's the Olympic Games," said Farmer John. "Wouldn't it be good to win a gold medal?"

"I bet," said Brian, "that if my animals were there they'd get one."

"Oh yeah?" said Farmer John. "If my animals were there they'd get ten!"

Wendy, Farmer John's wife, came in. "What are you arguing about now?" she laughed. "Perhaps you should have a 'games' of your own then, and you'd find out who was the best!"

"What a good idea," said Farmer John. "We could hold a competition here on Thistledown Farm!"

"OK," said Brian. "You're on. We'd better start training right away."

So Farmer John and Brian began training their animals for the competition. They set a date for the games, and decided what events the animals were going to compete in.

"Right," said Farmer John, when he had gathered everyone together. "Now, we've got two weeks to get fit for the big day. I want you Daisy to run round the big field twenty times after milking every morning."

"Mooo," said Daisy. "That sounds like hard work!"

"No pain no gain," said Farmer John. "If you want to win you'll have to put some effort in!"

So after milking next day, Daisy practised running around the field. She was very out of breath when she had finished. Farmer John timed her with his stopwatch. "That was OK," he said, "but I think you can do better."

"Mooo," said Daisy. "Why don't *you* run round the field and I'll time *you*!"

"But it's the Dairy Cow Dash!" said Farmer John. "It's not for farmers - it's for cows only."

"Oh well," said Daisy, "if you say so," and she galloped off around the field again.

Farmer John got the pigs, sheep and hens doing exercises every morning and every night after work, and they all began to get fitter and fitter and better and better at their events. They were all very keen to do well, and couldn't wait for the games to begin.

The night before the big day, Farmer John made everyone go to bed early. "Get a good night's sleep," he said, "it's an important day tomorrow. I want you all to be bright eyed and bushy tailed in the morning."

All the animals were very excited and they took a little while to get off to sleep, but when they did they slept like logs because they had all been training so hard.

The big day dawned and Farmer John sat up in bed. "Today's the day, Wendy!" he said. "Let's hope that all our hard work will pay off."

He dressed and went out to feed the animals. He gave them all a hearty breakfast, because they needed the energy. Brian arrived with his animals at one o'clock and the two teams limbered up, stretching their legs ready for the off.

"Now," said Farmer John. "The first event is the Sheep Hurdles." Mavis the ewe lined up on the starting line.

"BANG!" Farmer John's gun went off and the sheep sped off across the field.

"Go, Mavis, Go!" shouted the spectators, and everyone cheered and cheered. Mavis jumped the first fence. "Hooray!" the crowd shouted.

The sheep leapt over the hurdles, but at the last fence Mavis took a tumble. She fell over and the rest of the competitors all ran past. Brian's sheep came in first.

"Oh no," the crowd groaned. Mavis got up - she wasn't hurt at all.

Brian laughed to Farmer John, "That's the first race to me. You'll need to do better than that if you want to win."

"It's early days yet," said Farmer John. "Never mind Mavis...you did your best."

The next event was the Pigs' Pogo. All the pigs lined up. "BANG!" The gun went off. The pigs bounced down the field on their sticks.

57

"Come on Suzie!" shouted the crowd. Suzie the sow laughed as she hopped along. "WHEEE - what fun!" she cried. The crowd cheered and cheered and Suzie nearly fell off but she kept going, until right at the finishing line she hopped past one of Brian's pigs and came in first.

"HOORAY!" went the crowd, and Farmer John ran up and gave her a hug. "Well done, Suzie," he said.

"That's one all," he said to Brian. "Now you'd better look out!"

"There's plenty of time yet," said Brian.

"Now it's the Chicken Chase!" announced Farmer John.

All the birds lined up. "BANG!" Off went the hens. Round the field they sped, the crowd cheering them on. "Three laps," said Farmer John. "Hilda should do well." Hilda the hen was out in front.

"Go, Hilda, Go!" shouted the crowd, but just at the finishing line Hilda was overtaken by Reg the rooster, one of Brian's birds.

"Ha ha," laughed Brian. "I knew my birds were fitter than yours."

"Rubbish," said Farmer John. "You were just lucky!"

"Two-one to me," said Brian.

"Right," said Farmer John. "Now it's the Dairy Cow Dash."

All the cows lined up. "BANG!" went the gun. Daisy sped off down the field. Everyone laughed to see the cows galloping along like racehorses.

"Come on, Daisy!" the crowd shouted.

"MOOO," panted Daisy. "I'm going to win this." She was neck and neck with Brian's cows, but she put on a last spurt and crossed the line ahead by a nose.

"PHOTO FINISH!" said Farmer John. Everyone waited for the photo to come out. They all cheered when it was announced that Daisy was the winner.

"That's two all," said Farmer John. "We're even - we'll have to have a decider."

"I know," said Wendy, "why don't you have a tug of war?"

"Good idea!" said Farmer John. He went to the workshop and fetched a coil of rope.

"Now then, everyone," he said. "We want two teams - five for each side." So Brian chose four of his animals and so did Farmer John. They made two marks on the ground and tied a handkerchief to the middle of the rope.

"When I blow the whistle," said Wendy, "you can all pull."

PEEP! All the animals, Farmer John, and Brian dug their feet into the ground, and pulled for all they were worth. The hanky went one way and then the other.

"Heave!" said Farmer John.

"MOOO!" said Daisy.

"WHEEE!" said Suzie,

"BAAA!" said Mavis,

"CRAAWK!" went Hilda.

"We can do it," said Farmer John. "Pull, pull, pull!"

A trickle of sweat appeared on Farmer John's forehead; then, slowly, the hanky began to move towards the Thistledown Farm team, and inch by inch it crept closer towards the line.

"Go on," shouted Wendy. "Go on. You're nearly there!"

Farmer John made one last effort. His feet slipped and slithered in the mud - and suddenly Brian's team let go, and Farmer John and his animals all fell over.

"PEEP!" went Wendy. "WE'VE WON!"

"HOORAY!" went the crowd. Farmer John's team got up covered in mud, and shook hands with the other side.

"Well done, John," said Brian. "It was a close run thing, but I think you were the better side this time."

That evening Farmer John held a huge party to celebrate winning the games and all the animals, Farmer John, Brian and Wendy got very merry. From then on, every summer Farmer John and Brian held the Thistledown Farm Olympics to see whose animals were best!

FARMER JOHN'S TRUTH TONIC

Farmer John is feeling weak... but his tonic

has some unwanted side effects!

One bright morning Farmer John was having breakfast with Wendy, his wife. "I feel so *tired*," he complained, "I don't know why. Perhaps I'm working too hard." He sat and munched his bacon and eggs. He tried to lift a forkful of food to his mouth but he could hardly do it. "I'm so *weak*," he said. "I don't know what's wrong with me."

"Perhaps you need a tonic," said Wendy, "to help you get your strength back."

"That's a good idea," said Farmer John. "Do you think that it would work?"

"There's no harm in trying," said Wendy. "What's the worst that could happen?"

"That's true," said Farmer John. "Maybe I'll try it." He finished his coffee by lifting up the cup with both hands, struggled to the door, wrestled his boots on and tottered out into the yard.

The cows were being very difficult that morning and didn't want to be milked.

"Moo!" said Daisy. "Can't you hurry up? I've got lots of grass to eat today - time is precious, you know."

Farmer John groaned. "I'm going as fast as I can," he said. "I'm only human."

Daisy looked a bit concerned. "Are you all right?" she said. "You look a bit peaky, John - perhaps you need a rest."

"That would be very nice," said Farmer John, "but I have lots to do today. Hardworking farmers have to keep going, even when they feel tired."

Finally, Farmer John finished the milking, and he sat down for a breather. "Oh dear," he thought. "This is no good. I'll have to do better than this." He slowly got up and wobbled his way across to the feed store for a bag of pig food. He tried to lift the heavy bag, but it was no good. He had to get a trolley and wheeled the bag across to the pig pens.

"OINK! Morning, John," said Suzie. "You look a bit tired, what's wrong with you? Are you getting old?"

"I don't know," said Farmer John. "I feel like I'm a hundred, I can't lift anything. I think I've been working too hard."

"Oh dear," said Suzie. "Perhaps you need a holiday."

Farmer John snorted. "The chance would be a fine thing," he said. "I've got so much to do I can't afford a holiday - it's work, work, work for me, I'm afraid." He dragged the bag of pig food to the trough and filled it. "There you are," he said, "you won't go hungry this morning." Suzie gobbled up her breakfast.

At the sheep shed, Mavis was standing at the gate. "Baa!" she went. "Where's my breakfast? I'm huuungry."

"All right, all right, I'm coming," puffed Farmer John. He found a bale of hay, but he couldn't pick it up. He rolled it along the ground very slowly.

Mavis was surprised. "Have you lost your strength, John?" she asked.

"Yes," said Farmer John, "I've gone all weak and wobbly - I must have overdone it."

"You need a pick-me-up," said Mavis. "That would do the trick."

Farmer John groaned. "You're right," he said. "I think I'll get one right now." And he gave Mavis her hay, and weaved his way back to the farmhouse. He could barely walk in a straight line!

He was so tired that he couldn't be bothered to take his boots off in the porch. He crawled upstairs in his wellies, and collapsed on the bed - "Zzzzzzzzz..."

When he woke up, Wendy was shaking him. "John," she said, "wake up. I've got you something." Farmer John hauled himself up. "It's a tonic," said Wendy. "I've been to the chemists - they said it would be just the thing for you." Farmer John took the bottle. He unscrewed the cap and took a big swig. "Mmm," he said, "it tastes like blackcurrant." He took another swig, and another.

"I don't think you ought to have too much," said Wendy. "You don't know what effect it might have."

"Rubbish," said Farmer John, and he put the bottle to his lips and drank every last drop. "There," he said. "I'm feeling better already!"

"Oh dear," said Wendy. "I think you ought to be more careful -you never know what might happen with things you've never tried before. It could be dangerous."

"WENDY!" cried Farmer John. "I've never said this before, but you're always nagging. Nag, nag, nag, nag, nag...that's all you do. It's John Stubblefield this and John Stubblefield that - all you do is complain. I'm sick and tired of it. Why don't you find someone else to bother - I've got work to do." He jumped up and marched down the stairs.

Wendy was a little taken aback. "Goodness," she said. "I wonder what's got into *him*? All I said was that he ought to be more careful. Oh well...at least he seems to be feeling better." And she took the empty bottle and went downstairs.

Outside in the yard, Farmer John seemed to have the strength of ten men. He was rushing around carrying bales of hay, one on each arm, and heaving heavy sacks of pig food and fertilizer. He was running about with gates and drums of diesel, and everyone was quite alarmed!

"Goodness," said the pigs. "John seems to be back on form, but we've never seen him being this energetic. Wendy must have given him something good - I wonder what it is?"

Farmer John came over to the pig-pens and stared at them. "Hello, John," they said. "We see you've got your strength back then."

Farmer John looked at them. "I've never said this before," he said, "but I've never seen such a fat lot of pigs in my life. All you do is eat, eat, eat - you never do anything else. I give you my best pig food, and you just keep getting fatter. What a useless lot you are!"

The pigs opened their mouths in astonishment. "What on earth did he say that for?" said Suzie. "How rude". The pigs were very angry and upset!

In the field, Daisy was most surprised to have a visit from Farmer John.

"Daisy," said Farmer John, "I've never said this before, but you are so boring! All you do is eat grass and get milked. Every day, day in day out, morning and night, 365 days of the year. I'm fed up with you. You need to get a life." Daisy was speechless. But before she could answer, Farmer John had dashed off.

At the sheep shed, Mavis was nibbling some hay when Farmer John arrived. "Baa," said Mavis. "I see you're feeling better now, John."

Farmer John looked at Mavis. "I've never said this before," he said, "but you are the silliest sheep I've ever known. If there's an open gateway you won't go through it, but you'll push your way through the thickest hedge just because you think the grass looks a bit greener on the other side. I think you need your head looking at!"

He left Mavis looking bewildered. He was so busy the rest of the day that he didn't see anyone, and when he got back to the farmhouse it was getting dark. He was just about to open the door when he was confronted by Wendy and all the animals.

"JOHN STUBBLEFIELD," they cried. "We've never said this before - but we think you're the rudest farmer in the county!"

Suzie stepped forward. "You told me that I was fat and lazy," she said.

"And you told me that I was boring," said Daisy.

"And you told me that I needed my head looking at," said Mavis.

"And you said," added Wendy, "that I was always nagging. What have you got to say for yourself?"

Farmer John looked shocked. "Oh dear," he said. "Did I really say that? I didn't really mean it. I wonder why that was?"

"I think I know the answer," said Wendy, and she got out the empty bottle of tonic. "It says here," she said, looking at the label, "that if you drink too much it makes you say what you think. You drank the whole bottle - no wonder you were so rude. You were lucky much worse didn't happen!"

Farmer John grinned sheepishly. "I'd better make sure I read the label next time," he said. "It's good to be honest but sometimes it's not always a good idea to say exactly what you think at the time...it can get you into trouble."

"Yes," said Wendy. "In future I think you'd better have just a teaspoonful...that should be quite enough to keep your strength up."

So from then on whenever Farmer John felt a bit tired he took just a little tonic; because although he knew that honesty is the best policy, he also knew that the truth is often best kept to yourself!

FARMER JOHN'S OVERALLS

Farmer John buys himself a new pair of overalls - but he has difficulty keeping them clean!

One bright morning, Farmer John climbed out of bed and reached for his clothes. "Oh what a beautiful morning!" he said to Wendy his wife. "I've got a wonderful feeling everything's going my way."

Wendy laughed. "You *are* in a good mood," she said.

"Yes," said Farmer John. "Nothing's going to go wrong today...I can feel it in my bones."

"Really?" said Wendy, "I'm *so* glad - you're usually making a mess of something or other."

"Rubbish!" said Farmer John. "I'm just a bit unlucky sometimes, that's all. Anyway, today's going to be different. You'll see."

They dressed and went downstairs for breakfast. When they had finished, Farmer John looked for his overalls on the peg.

"Where have my overalls gone?" he said to Wendy. "I can't find them anywhere."

"Oh, I threw them out," said Wendy. "They were in such a state! You must have had them for ages - it's time you got yourself a new pair."

"Huh," said Farmer John. "Thanks for telling me. I'd better go to the stores." And he hopped into Lawrence the Landrover and drove off. When he got there he looked through all the clothes.

"Waterproof jackets - no, I've got those," he muttered. "Boots – no, I've got those. Ah - here we are." There, on a shelf, were packets of overalls. There were red ones and green ones and blue ones. "Hmm," he thought, "now what colour shall I choose?"

He was just about to take a pair of nice blue ones when his eye fell on a packet by his head. "Wow," he said. "White! I've never had a pair of white overalls before. They look really smart; I must have them." He took them to the counter.

The salesman looked at him. "Hello John," he said. "Buying new overalls, are we?"

"Yes," said Farmer John. "Wendy threw my old ones out."

"Unusual choice of colour, John" said the salesman. "Are you sure you don't want a nice pair of blue ones?"

"No," said Farmer John. "I want some white ones for a change - they'll be very smart. Everyone will be able to see me coming."

"That's true," said the salesman. "Here's your change." And Farmer John hurried out of the shop.

He rushed back to the farm to feed his animals, and pulled on his new overalls. They gleamed a shiny white in the sun. "Right," he said, "let's get to work."

The sheep were in the field when he came in through the gate with a big bag of sheep feed. "Baa," they all cried. "Food! Let's go, girls!" They all rushed towards Farmer John in a mob.

"STOP!" cried Farmer John. "I haven't opened the bag yet!" But it was too late; the sheep all pushed against Farmer John's legs. They shoved and heaved and Farmer John fell over - SQUELCH! -in the muddy gateway. His feedbag went flying.

"Oh my goodness," he cried, "you naughty sheep! Look at my nice clean overalls...they're covered in mud!"

"Baa," the sheep bleated. "Sorry, John, but we were so huuungry! We won't do that again."

"Hmph," said Farmer John. "You'd better not, or else." He got up and looked at himself. "I don't think white was such a good colour to choose for farm work," he said.

He toddled off down to the pig-pens. "Here's your grub," he said and poured a bag of barley into the trough. The pigs came running out. "What's happened to your nice white overalls, John?" they said. "It looks like you've had an accident."

"The sheep knocked me over in the mud," grumbled Farmer John.

"Aha!" cried the pigs. "We can do better than that..." and they began to throw yucky muck at him!

"NO," cried Farmer John, "DON'T!" But it was too late - his overalls had huge mucky brown stains on them. "You cheeky lot!" he said. "If you ever do that again you'll go without food for a week."

"Sorry John," said the pigs, "but we couldn't resist it."

"Huh," said Farmer John. "I'm off to see the cows."

Daisy the dairy cow was in the cow barn when Farmer John arrived.

"Hello Daisy," said Farmer John. "I just want you to give me a bucket of milk to feed the calves...I won't be a minute." He got a bucket, and crouched down by Daisy's udder. He started to pull at Daisy's teats, and soon the bucket was brimful of warm milk. Daisy was a bit ticklish. She kicked the bucket of milk and it went flying, splashing sticky milk all over Farmer Johns' overalls.

"YUCK!" cried Farmer John. "What did you do that for?"

"You were tickling me," said Daisy.

"Now look what you've done," said Farmer John crossly. "As if my overalls weren't messy enough! If you do that again, you'll be in trouble."

"OK," said Daisy, "but don't tickle me next time."

Farmer John was a bit fed up. His nice white overalls were covered in mud and muck and milk, and they were wet and soggy.

"Now, what else do I have to do?" he asked himself. "Ah yes - my tractor." He marched over to the tractor shed. "Now hold still Tommy," he said, "this won't take a minute. I just have to change your oil."

He undid Tommy's oil plug, but instead of the oil dripping out it squirted all over him.

"Aaargh," cried Farmer John. "Look what you've done now!"

Tommy laughed. "I'm sorry, but I couldn't resist it! I'm doing you a favour - a farmer isn't a farmer without oil on his overalls."

"Grrumph!" said Farmer John. "I suppose you think that was funny, but I don't. If that happens again you won't get any diesel for a week."

"Oh dear," said Tommy. "It was only a joke."

"Well, I'm not laughing," said Farmer John, and he marched back to the farmhouse.

Wendy was in the kitchen, doing her washing. "Look at you," she laughed, "what *have* you been up to? I knew those white overalls wouldn't last five minutes."

"Huh," grunted Farmer John, "everyone's been having great fun making them messy - can you wash them for me?"

"OK," said Wendy. "Pop them in - I'm just doing a load now."

Farmer John put them in the washing machine and Wendy turned it on. "They won't be long," she said. "When they're finished I'll put them in the dryer, and you can have them this afternoon." So Farmer John went and had his lunch and a nap and soon his overalls were ready.

"Here they are, John," said Wendy, holding them up.

Farmer John's jaw dropped. "Wh-wh-WHAT!" he stuttered - his overalls were bright pink! "But they've turned pink," he cried.

Wendy laughed. "Yes," she said, "I put them in with my red knickers, but never mind - they're clean, at least."

"But I can't wear pink overalls!" cried Farmer John.

"You'll have to this afternoon," said Wendy. "You haven't any other pairs."

"Oh dear," said Farmer John. "But everyone will laugh at me."

"That makes no difference," said Wendy, "they do anyway!"

Farmer John put on his pink overalls in a huff. He walked up to see his sheep.

The sheep whistled. "Very nice John," they said. "Is that the new fashion?"

"No, it's not," said Farmer John. "Wendy put them in with her red panties, and now I feel like a right idiot."

"No you don't," said the sheep, "you look lovely. HA HA!"

"I know," said Farmer John, "can you knock me over in the mud again? That would cover up the colour."

"Sorry, John," said the sheep. "You told us not to do that again."

"Please!" begged Farmer John.

"No can do," bleated the sheep.

Farmer John went to the pigs. "Can you throw muck at me again?" he pleaded.

The pigs laughed. "What, and spoil those nice pink overalls?" they said. "How could we? Anyway, you said we wouldn't get fed for a week if we did it again."

"Oh drat," said Farmer John, and he went off to see Daisy.

"MOO!" said Daisy. "Very fetching, but you need a pair of pink boots to go with them."

"HO HO HO," said Farmer John, "you are *so* not funny. Can you cover me in milk if I get a bucket?"

"No!" said Daisy. "You said there would be trouble if I did that again."

Farmer John was getting desperate. "I know," he said. "I'll try Tommy." Tommy was standing in the tractor shed, talking to Myrtle the muck-spreader. They both looked up. "You're looking in the pink today, John," they said, and burst into guffaws of laughter.

Farmer John went bright red. "Please help me," he said. "Can you cover them in oil like you did this morning?"

"Well, I'd love to," said Tommy, "but you said I wouldn't get diesel for a week if I did that again. Anyway, why do you want to spoil them? Pink suits you...it goes with your eyes."

Farmer John blushed. "No it doesn't," he said. "Blue's my colour. Well - if you won't help me, I'll have to help myself."

So, when no-one was looking, Farmer John found a nice quiet field and rolled around in a big muddy patch. He stood up. He could still see bits of pink. He marched over to the muck heap and sat in it. Then he got a bucketful of milk from the dairy and tipped it over his head, and finally he found an old can of black oil in the workshop and poured it over his shoulders.

"There," he said satisfied. "No-one can tell I'm wearing pink overalls now," and he marched back to the farmhouse.

Wendy was making tea. "Goodness," she said, "you've done it again! Just give them to me and I'll pop them in the wash."

"No fear," said Farmer John hastily. "I think I'll wear them like this from now on."

"But they stink," said Wendy.

"Yes," said Farmer John, "but I think it's better to stink than to wear pink, don't you?"

Wendy laughed. "OK," she said, "but perhaps you'd better go and get yourself a nice blue pair tomorrow - I don't think I could put up with the smell!"

So Farmer John went and bought himself a pair of blue overalls the next day. The salesman asked him if he wouldn't prefer a pink pair, because the story of Farmer Johns' overalls had spread far and wide. "You've started a new fashion, John," he said. "Every farmer in the county has been coming in asking for pink overalls - it's been causing great amusement!"

Eventually Wendy got fed up and washed Farmer John's overalls, and there they hung on the peg in the porch, waiting for the day for pink to become fashionable for farmers!

FARMER JOHN'S RHUBARB RACKET

Farmer John hatches a good wheeze to make a little money!

It was a bright morning on Thistledown Farm and Farmer John was helping himself to a big breakfast. He piled six sausages, five rashers of bacon, four eggs, three tomatoes, two slices of fried bread and a large mushroom onto his plate.

He sat down and began to eat. Wendy, his wife, came in. "You greedy pig," she said. "Look at all that fried food - it's not good for you. Besides, we can't afford it!"

Farmer John frowned. "Am I short of money again?" he said. "I thought we borrowed some from the bank manager. Has it all gone?"

"Yes," said Wendy. "We'll have to borrow some more if you keep eating your way through our profits like that."

"Oh dear," said Farmer John, munching slowly. "We'll have to tighten our belts."

"By the look of you," said Wendy, "you'll have to let your belt out a couple of holes. You're getting plump."

"But I have to eat," he said. "Hardworking farmers need feeding, just like their animals."

"Well," said Wendy. "You'd better do something to bring in more money, or we'll be out of business."

Farmer John pondered. "I know," he said. "I'll nip off to market and see if I can find any bargains." So he hopped into Lawrence the Landrover, and buzzed off to market.

There were lots of stallholders showing off their wares and drovers shouting and cattle mooing and sheep bleating when he arrived. "What a noisy place," thought Farmer John. "I wonder what I can find."

He walked along the stalls. Someone was selling rabbits and hamsters, someone was selling clothes, another was selling pies and another cakes. He came to a man in a cap who had a stall full of plants.

"Those are interesting," said Farmer John to the man. "I've never seen plants like those before...what are they?"

"They're rhubarb plants," said the man. "Put them in now and they'll make you a lot of money."

"Really?" said Farmer John excitedly. "I'll take the lot!"

He gathered all the pots together in his arms, paid the man and tottered off back to Lawrence. The rhubarb plants filled the back of the Landrover and he had to put the rest on the seat next to him; they poked through the window as he drove along. It looked like he was transporting a hedge!

When he got back to the farm, Wendy was waiting for him. "What have you got there?" she laughed. "A jungle?"

"You can laugh," said Farmer John, "but these plants are the answer to our money problems - you'll see."

He spent the rest of the day planting them out in the big field. He paced up and down, digging holes with a spade and popping each plant in carefully, spacing them out until the whole field was covered in rhubarb plants. "There," he said when he had finished. "With a bit of rain and a bit of muck they will soon grow well."

He was quite tired when he went to bed that night. His back was aching a little from stooping over, and he soon fell sound asleep. When he woke up the next morning he was quite excited.

"I wonder how my rhubarb is getting on?" he thought, and rushed out without any breakfast to go and look.

He marched up the lane to the big field...but where was the big field? He stood at the gate and stared. His jaw dropped. There was a tangled jungle of massive rhubarb plants towering above him. The stalks were like tree trunks and the leaves like huge green umbrellas.

"Gosh," he said. "I didn't think those plants would grow so quickly. I must have put too much muck on them. Oh dear - what am I going to do with all this rhubarb?"

He rushed back to the farmhouse. "Wendy," he said. "Do you like rhubarb crumble?"

"Oh yes," said Wendy.

"Well," said Farmer John, "we have enough to last us a life time."

"Oh dear," said Wendy. "What have you done now?"

"My rhubarb crop has grown extra large," said Farmer John. "What shall I do?"

"Why not feed it to the cows?" said Wendy.

"Good idea," said Farmer John. So he got a pith helmet and a knife and began hacking through the rhubarb jungle. He filled a trailer and drove it down to the cows. "Here you are," he said. "Try this - it's very good for you."

The cows nibbled the rhubarb. "Moo," they said, "it makes a change from grass I suppose," and they tucked in. It wasn't long though before they were moaning and groaning and clutching their stomachs.

"What's wrong?" said Farmer John, alarmed.

"We've got tummy ache," the cows moaned. "It's all that rhubarb, it's making us feel sick."

"Oh dear," said Farmer John. "Stay there and I'll fetch the vet."

Mr. Young the vet was a very old man. He came into the yard in his smart red car. "What's the problem, John?" he said.

"My cows have eaten too much rhubarb," said Farmer John. "They're feeling ill."

"Have you given them any custard?" asked the vet.

"No," said Farmer John. "Is that necessary?"

"Of course," said Mr. Young. "You always serve rhubarb with custard."

So Wendy mixed up some custard and Farmer John poured it into the feed troughs. The cows drank it up. "Moo," they said. "That's better!"

Farmer John was relieved, but he still had a problem. He had loads of rhubarb left to get rid of. "Do you want any?" he asked the vet.

"No thank you, John," laughed Mr. Young. "I've got quite a lot in my own garden, but I think I may have an idea which might help you."

Farmer John listened to Mr. Young's idea. "That sounds good," he said, and got to work. He painted a sign saying "Pick your own Rhubarb: Ten pounds per bag," and put it at the end of his lane.

Soon lots of people drove up to pick the rhubarb. Farmer John gave them sacks and a knife and they happily hacked the giant rhubarb down. By the end of the day most of the field had gone and Farmer John had a great wodge of ten-pound notes in his pocket.

"What are you going to do with all that money, John?" asked Wendy.

"I'm going to pay back the money I owe the bank manager and take us on holiday," said Farmer John. "You deserve a break."

Farmer John grew rhubarb every year from then on, until all the animals got quite sick of it and persuaded him to grow strawberries instead!

FARMER JOHN'S MATING SEASON

All Farmer John's animals are having relationship

problems...but Farmer John acts as Cupid!

One November morning Farmer John woke up and stretched. He yawned and opened his eyes. "It looks like a nice day outside," he said to Wendy his wife. "I wonder what's going to happen today?"

"I don't know," said Wendy, "but knowing you, something will."

Farmer John laughed. "You're right," he said. "Something's always going on at Thistledown Farm - but it always turns out right in the end."

They dressed and went downstairs for breakfast. Farmer John tucked into his bacon and eggs. "I've been thinking, Wendy," he said, in between mouthfuls. "It's time the ram went in with the ewes. If he doesn't go in now we won't have any lambs next spring. The ram needs to mate with the ewes if we're to have any lambs born."

"That's right," said Wendy, "and the bull needs to go with the cows to get some calves next autumn, and the boar needs to mate with the sows so we can have some piglets, and we need some new chicks to hatch out - the cockerel must go with the hens to make them broody."

Farmer John nodded. "I think that our animals need to start thinking about romance," he said. "We need to get them in the mood for love."

Wendy laughed. "We were in the mood for love before Johnny and Jemima were born," she said. "Do you remember?"

"Yes," said Farmer John. "It was our wedding night. We were very romantic - we had candles and soft music."

"That's right," said Wendy. "Then nine months later Johnny and Jemima came along; isn't it wonderful?"

"My twins are the best thing that's happened to me," said Farmer John. "Apart from meeting you of course, my dear," he added hastily.

Farmer John finished his breakfast and went out into the yard to see his animals. He marched down to the pig-pens. Suzie the sow was scratching herself on the wall. "Morning Suzie," he said cheerfully. "What a beautiful day. It puts you in the mood for love, doesn't it!"

"OINK!" said Suzie. "Love? What's that?"

Farmer John was a little taken aback. "Doesn't this weather make you feel loving?" he asked.

"No, it doesn't," said Suzie. "I don't love anyone - it's stuff and nonsense."

"Oh dear," said Farmer John. "What's wrong with you today?"

"Brendan the boar has been mean to me," she said.

"Why?" asked Farmer John.

"I don't know," said Suzie, "but if he's going to be like that, I don't love him any more."

"Oh," said Farmer John. "I'm sure there's a good explanation -leave it to me."

Farmer John went over to the bull pen. "Morning, Hercules," he said. "Lovely day isn't it? Puts you in the mood for love...how's Daisy?"

"Daisy!" Hercules snorted. "I don't love that cow - she's been talking to another bull!"

"Oh dear," said Farmer John. "I'm sure she doesn't mean anything by it. She's probably just being friendly."

"Pah!" said Hercules. "She hasn't talked to me for ages. I feel hurt."

"Never mind, Hercules," said Farmer John. "Let me see what I can do."

Farmer John shook his head. He was a little worried about his animals...they didn't seem to be getting on very well together. "Oh well," he said, and toddled off to see his sheep. Mavis the ewe was looking quite unhappy.

"Don't tell me," said Farmer John, "you've got boyfriend problems."

"How did you know?" bleated Mavis.

"I'm an expert when it comes to affairs of the heart," said Farmer John knowingly. "Everyone comes to me with their problems. Now, how can I help you?"

"Well," said Mavis. "The ram isn't paying me enough attention, he's always with the other ewes. What can I do?"

"Hmm," said Farmer John, "that's a tricky one. I'll think about it and come back to you."

Farmer John left Mavis and went across to the chicken run. Hilda the hen was sitting on the fence looking very sad. "Not you as well!" said Farmer John. "I can tell just by looking at you – you're having relationship problems."

Hilda wiped a tear from her eye. "Cedric and I have fallen out," she said. "We're not speaking to each other. We had a huge row and now I'm very unhappy."

"Oh you don't want to worry about that cockerel," said Farmer John. "He's such a bighead - Cedric's always arguing about something."

"But he said some very nasty things," moaned Hilda, "and I'm very upset."

"Well," said Farmer John, "I'm good at sorting out problems. Leave it to me, and we'll soon get you two back together."

Farmer John went back to the farmhouse. "Goodness," he said to Wendy, "my animals *are* having a rough time -

they've all fallen out! Brendan the boar is being mean to Suzie the sow, Hercules the bull doesn't like Daisy the dairy cow any more, Reg the ram is ignoring Mavis the ewe and Hilda the hen and Cedric the cockerel have had cross words."

"Deary me," said Wendy. "We're not going to get any lambs, calves, piglets or chicks if this carries on. What are we going to do?"

"I'm working on it," said Farmer John. "I need to put my thinking cap on." He went into his office and closed the door. He came out a little while later with a smile on his face.

"Any luck?" asked Wendy.

Farmer John nodded. "I have a cunning plan," he said. "We'll soon get those animals talking again."

He slipped his boots on and went over to the boar pen. Brendan was munching away at his trough. "Hello John," he said. "What can I do for you?"

"Well," said Farmer John, "Suzie says you're being mean to her. Why's that?"

"Because I don't think she loves me," said Brendan.

"She might love you if you gave her some flowers," said Farmer John.

"Really?" said Brendan, brightening up. "Do you think so?

"Here," said Farmer John. "Take these petunias, and go and give them to her."

So Brendan trotted off and delivered the petunias to Suzie. She sniffed at them. "Aaah!" she said. "Flowers, how lovely! Oh thank you, Brendan," and gave him a big sloppy kiss. Farmer John was pleased - his plan was working!

He walked across to the cow yard. "Hello Daisy," he said. "I hear Hercules doesn't love you anymore because you've been talking to another bull."

Daisy laughed. "Oh he's just a friend," she said. "I don't feel anything for him."

"Well," said Farmer John, "why don't you write a love note to Hercules. I'm sure he'd love you again if you did that."

So Daisy sat down and wrote a love note. It said: *Darling Hercules, you're the only one for me. I only have eyes for you. Love Daisy.* She trotted over to the bull pen and handed it over. Hercules read the note. "Daisy," he cried, "I didn't know you cared." They both embraced. Farmer John rubbed his hands together; things were going nicely.

At the sheep shed, Mavis was still moping around. "Here," said Farmer John, "I've got an idea for you," and he whispered in Mavis's ear. Mavis suddenly clutched her stomach. "Ooh," she groaned. "I feel so unwell."

Reg the ram came running. "What's the matter, Mavis?" he asked.

"I'm feeling poorly...please look after me."

Reg cuddled up to Mavis. "Don't worry," he said soothingly, "I'm here for you."

Mavis winked at Farmer John. "Ooh," she said, "don't leave me!"

"I'm not going anywhere," said Reg. "You're everything to me." Farmer John smiled. Love was in the air.

He crossed the yard to the chicken coop. "Cedric," he called. "I want a word with you." Cedric came running.

"What's up, John?" he panted.

"Just pop inside the coop for a minute," said Farmer John. "I want to show you something."

So Cedric hopped inside the chicken coop. It was empty inside. "What do you want to show me?" said Cedric.

"Wait there," said Farmer John. He picked up Hilda and popped her inside the coop and shut the door. "Now they can sort out their differences by themselves," said Farmer John. He listened at the door. He heard Hilda crying, then he heard Cedric telling her not to cry and when he opened the door both birds had their wings around each other, cuddling.

Farmer John was overjoyed. "Success!" he said. "All my animals are back together again," and he rushed back to the house to tell Wendy the good news.

After that everyone was very happy, and it wasn't long before the sound of bleating lambs, squealing piglets, mooing calves and cheeping chicks could be heard on Thistledown Farm!

FARMER JOHN'S OSTRICH FARM

Farmer John decides to go in for Ostrich farming, but

things don't quite go according to plan…

It was breakfast time on Thistledown Farm, and Farmer John was talking to Wendy, his wife. "Things aren't looking too good," he said. "We're not making enough money. I may have to start selling some of my animals."

"Oh dear," said Wendy. "We can't do that. Isn't there anything you can do?"

"I don't know," said Farmer John. "I'll have to put my thinking cap on." He sat and read the farming paper as he sipped his cup of tea. Suddenly, he sat up. "Look at this!" he said. "It's an article about Ostriches."

"Really?" said Wendy. "What does it say?"

"It says that Ostrich farming is the new growth industry," said Farmer John. "Lots of people are keeping them these days - apparently they're a real money spinner."

"What do you have to do?" said Wendy

"I don't know," said Farmer John. "It doesn't really say. It says their tail feathers are beautiful and very valuable, though. Perhaps we should buy some birds - we've got some savings."

"I think you need to be careful," said Wendy. "You don't know anything about keeping ostriches."

"Rubbish!" said farmer John. "It can't be that difficult. I know all about farming; I don't need any books to tell me what to do."

"Well, I'm not sure," said Wendy. "It seems like a big risk to me."

"Nonsense," said Farmer John. "I think ostriches are the answer to all our prayers. We're going to make our fortunes...I can see it now!"

"Well, if that's what you want to do," said Wendy. "But don't say I didn't warn you!"

Farmer John finished his breakfast and went out into the yard. He marched across to the cow yard. Daisy the dairy cow was standing by the water trough. "Moo!" she said. "Morning John, how are you today?"

"I'm fine," said Farmer John. "I'm just about to become very rich indeed."

"Really?" said Daisy. "Has somebody left you something, then?"

"No," said Farmer John, "but I'm going into ostriches - they're the next big thing."

"Goodness!" said Daisy. "Are you sure you know what you're doooing?"

"Absolutely," said Farmer John. "It's as easy as falling off a log - it's going to be the end of all my money worries. I won't have to sell any of you cows now."

"Moo," said Daisy. "Thank goodness for that!"

Farmer John toddled up to the sheep shed. Mavis the ewe was chewing some hay in the corner.

"Morning, Mavis," said Farmer John cheerfully. "How are you today?"

"Baa" said Mavis, "not baaad. What's this I hear about you keeping ostriches, John?"

"Gosh!" said Farmer John. "News travels fast around here. Well, I've found a way to make a lot of money, so I won't have to sell any of you sheep now."

"Baa," said Mavis. "That's good - but aren't ostriches difficult to keep, John?"

"Not at all," said Farmer John, "it couldn't be easier. I'm going to order some today." He pushed off to see the pigs.

Suzie the sow was scratching herself on the pig-pen wall when Farmer John arrived.

"Morning, Suzie!" said Farmer John. "I've got news for you."

"Yes," said Suzie, "you're going to order some ostriches today."

"Goodness," said Farmer John. "How does gossip get around my farm so fast? It must be the mice! Yes, I just thought I'd let you know I can keep all you pigs on, now. My new ostrich farm is going to be a huge success."

"OINK!" said Suzie. "I hope so, John - but do you know much about ostriches?"

"Well...not really," said Farmer John. "But it can't be that difficult - lots of people are keeping them these days. Anything they can do I can do better!" He toddled off back to the farmhouse.

He looked in the phone book under 'O' for Ostriches, and soon found a number. He rang up and ordered fifty ostriches to be delivered that day. He rubbed his hands together as he put down the phone. "I'm in the money, I'm in the money!" he sang, as he sat down to his lunch.

Wendy laughed. "You haven't got them yet!" she said. "Don't you think you're counting your chickens before they're hatched?"

"Who said anything about chickens?" said Farmer John. "It's ostriches I'm talking about!"

"Well, don't count your *ostriches* before they are hatched," said Wendy, and she gave him a plate of his favourite beef stew.

After lunch Farmer John had a little nap, but was soon woken by the sound of a lorry pulling into the yard. He jumped into his boots and rushed out. "Have you got my ostriches?" he said excitedly to the driver.

"Yep, sure have," said the driver. "Where do you want them?"

Farmer John puzzled. "I haven't really thought about it," he said. "Perhaps we'd better put them in a field." So the driver reversed up the lane to a gateway, let down the tailboard, and a flock of fifty great big ostriches ran out.

"Gosh," said Farmer John, "I didn't realise ostriches were so big! What am I going to do with this lot?"

"I dunno," said the driver. "That's your problem!" He closed the tailgate, and drove off.

Farmer John closed the gate and looked at all his new birds. They stared back at him. They didn't look too friendly!

"Oh dear," thought Farmer John. "Perhaps I should have learned more about them...but never mind. I've got them now." He looked at their tail feathers; they did look very beautiful. "I wonder if I could gather some?" thought Farmer John. "Hmmm..."

He climbed over the gate, and tried to get near one of the birds. He got very close, grabbed hold of its tail and pulled. A handful of feathers came away in his hands. Farmer John was so pleased that he didn't see the bird turn round and nip him on the bottom with its big beak!

"OUCH, OUCH, OUCH!" cried Farmer John. He backed off, but the bird wasn't going to let him get away. It began to chase Farmer John across the field. She was a very good runner and Farmer John had to move extra fast to keep away from her snapping beak.

All the other birds joined in the chase and Farmer John leapt over the hedge just in the nick of time. "Phew!" he thought. "Nasty birds! I only want a few of their tail feathers - surely that's not too much to ask?"

But he wasn't prepared for what happened next. He didn't know that ostriches need tall fences to keep them in, and the birds climbed over the hedge and began to chase him back to the farmyard! Poor Farmer John - he was terrified of all those snapping beaks behind him! He got very out of breath by the time he reached the farmyard, and had to climb up on to the cow-barn roof to get away. The ostriches ran around in all directions below.

"HELP, HELP!" cried Farmer John.

Wendy heard him and came running. "JOHN STUBBLEFIELD -what *are* you doing up there?" she called.

"Save me!" said Farmer John. "My ostriches are attacking me!"

Wendy burst out laughing. "I warned you something like this would happen!" she said. "Stay there, and I'll see what I can do."

She got a big bag of corn from the feed-store and poured a trail of seeds from the farmyard up to the sheep shed. All the birds followed the trail, pecking at the corn until they were all inside the shed, opposite the sheep. Wendy closed the door on them and shut them inside. "It's quite safe," she said to Farmer John. "You can come down now."

"Are you sure?" said Farmer John; he was very sore. He climbed down. He showed Wendy the ostrich feathers he had taken.

"I'm not surprised they turned on you," said Wendy. "I don't think I'd like feathers plucked out of my bottom!"

Just then, PC Collar drove into the yard in his smart police car. He squeezed himself out. "Is this your bird, sir?" he asked. He had an ostrich in the back seat!

"Yes officer," said Farmer John. "I think it is."

"Well, I had to arrest it for going the wrong way down a motorway," said the policeman. "Do you have a licence for it, sir?"

"I don't think so," said Farmer John.

"Well I'm afraid I'm going to have to give you a ticket in that case. Perhaps you could keep your birds under control in future?"

"Yes officer, thank you officer," said Farmer John. PC Collar wrote him out a ticket, and drove off.

"Well," said Wendy, "we'd better put this one with the others."

The sheep were very interested in the ostriches and where they came from. "We come from darkest Africa," said the ostriches, "and we are renowned for running fast and sticking our heads in the sand."

"Really?" said the sheep. "That's a bit silly, isn't it?"

"Not half as silly as you look!" said the ostriches.

Farmer John soon got busy building a tall fence around the big field. He wasn't going to let his birds get loose again! It wasn't long before they all began to lay eggs, and he had lots of little baby ostriches running around. He decided it was too risky trying to pull the birds' tail feathers, and instead he charged visitors five pounds each to come and look at them.

Farmer John didn't make his fortune with his ostriches, but he did make enough money to save his animals from being sold. They were very happy - and because his animals were happy, Farmer John was happy too!

FARMER JOHN'S BULL

Hercules the bull helps Farmer John deal with a group of rude ramblers!

One fine morning, Farmer John jumped out of bed and pulled back the curtains. "What a lovely day," he said to Wendy, his wife. "It's the weekend. I expect there'll be lots of people out walking today. I'd better go and make sure the footpath is clear."

He had his breakfast, then went into the workshop and got a sharp sickle and walked up the lane to the footpath. It went through the field of sheep, across a field with some cows in, round the edge of a field of wheat and down to the river field where a bull was grazing.

Farmer John started to cut back the overgrown brambles and thistles, thorns and nettles along the footpath. He whistled a cheerful tune as he worked away. It was quite pleasant in the sunshine and he soon had company. Groups of happy walkers came along the footpath and stopped and passed a cheery word with him.

They came from all over the country and were very interested in Thistledown Farm. Farmer John told them all about his animals and the things they got up to. The walkers enjoyed listening to Farmer John's stories and were a bit sad when they said good-bye. All morning people came past in ones or twos or in groups and stopped to talk, or greeted him politely and walked on. Farmer John was really enjoying his morning's work, when something happened to spoil it all.

A troop of noisy ramblers in coloured jackets and walking boots came strolling up the path. "Morning," said Farmer John merrily. The ramblers looked at him and laughed. "Oh look, it's a farmer. How quaint."

Farmer John stopped smiling. "Look," said one of the ramblers, "he's doing manual work. Let's not talk to *him*," and the group marched past Farmer John without even saying hello.

Farmer John was not very happy. "How rude!" he said. "They think that I'm beneath them because I work with my hands. How ignorant. I'm not sure they're the sort of people I want walking across *my* farm," and he swiped at a thistle crossly with his sickle.

He was just about to go home for lunch when he noticed that the sheep were out. They had escaped from the field they were supposed to be in. "Bother," said Farmer John, and he ran across to put them back. He got very out of breath and cross with chasing them around, and they took a long time to go back where they belonged.

"Those ramblers left the gate open!" said Farmer John angrily. "Don't they know the country code? I'd better see what other damage they've done."

He walked along and came to a pile of crisp packets, sweet wrappers and beer bottles. "Look what they've left behind," he said. "Don't they know not to leave litter? It can be dangerous for animals and birds." He picked up all the litter and put it in a bag.

"Right," he said, "and now for some lunch." But when he looked back, he saw that the rambler's dog was chasing his cows around in the field across the way.

"Grr!" Farmer John was very angry. "Those wretched ramblers, don't they know to keep their dogs on a lead?" he said. Then when he looked again he saw that the ramblers had strayed from the footpath and had walked through his wheat, flattening it down. They were now spreading themselves out in it and having a picnic!

"That's it!" said Farmer John. "I've had enough. I'm going to deal with this!" He hopped over the hedge and crossed a couple of fields until he came to the one with the bull in it.

"Now then, Hercules," he said. "There's something you can do for me..." He took a sign off the gate saying BEWARE OF THE BULL, and hid it in the hedge.

"There," said Farmer John. "Let's see what becomes of those thoughtless ramblers now." He sat down and hid himself behind a bush.

After a while, the rude ramblers came along. "Look, let's go through this field," they said. "It's a short cut." They climbed over the gate and went in.

Hercules the bull was standing beside the fence. "Look, it's a cow," said one of the ramblers.

Hercules was most offended. "Me? A cow? I'll show them!" He let out a huge bellow.

"I d-d-don't think it's a cow," said another rambler. "I think it's a bull!"

"A bull?" They all began to tremble. "Run for it," one of them cried, and he started to race across the field. Hercules soon caught up with him, and tossed him through the air!

The rambler landed – "OUCH!" - in a prickly holly bush. All the other ramblers split up and ran in all directions. Hercules chased after them and one landed - SPLOSH! - in the river, another landed head first in a badger's sett, his legs sticking in the air, and another ended up clinging to the branch of a tree. The last one was thrown over the hedge and landed - SQUELCH! - in a pile of manure!

Farmer John laughed at them. "That'll teach you all to ignore the country code!" he said. "Here, take this home with you," and he handed them their bag of rubbish. The ramblers were very sorry and apologised to Farmer John for being so rude, and said they would be better next time.

Farmer John gave Hercules a pat on the neck. "Well done," he said, "but don't go doing that all the time."

Farmer John put up a sign at the end of his lane saying WALKERS WELCOME – PLEASE REMEMBER THE COUNTRY CODE, and from then on everyone who came to walk through Thistledown Farm was very good. The ramblers learnt their lesson, and were never so thoughtless again!

FARMER JOHN'S DIET

**Farmer John goes on a strict diet - but
his animals catch him with his face
in the fridge!**

One morning Farmer John climbed out of bed and reached for his clothes. He looked down. "I can't see my feet," he said to Wendy his wife.

Wendy laughed. "That's because you're getting plump," she said. "You eat too much!"

Farmer John frowned. "But I need to keep my strength up," he said. "Hard-working farmers need to feed themselves, just like their animals."

Wendy laughed. "Your animals are getting too plump as well," she said. "Perhaps you need to go on a diet."

"Maybe you're right," said Farmer John. "We could do with losing a few pounds. It would be good for us."

They dressed and went downstairs for breakfast. Farmer John piled his plate with bacon, eggs, sausages, tomatoes, fried bread, beans and mushrooms. He sat down, but just as he was about to put a forkful into his mouth, Wendy whisked the plate away from under his nose.

"HEY!" said Farmer John. "I haven't finished!"

Wendy emptied the breakfast into the bin. "You can't eat that," she said. "Fried food isn't good for you. Your diet starts right now," and she gave Farmer John a piece of dry toast and a glass of water. "There," she said, "that's your rations for this morning!"

Farmer John was not impressed. "You can't expect me to go to work on a piece of dry toast!" he complained.

Wendy laughed. "If you're serious about losing weight, you'll have to eat what I give you," she said.

Farmer John grumbled, "Oh all right, but I'll need something better for my lunch," and he tottered out to feed his animals. Daisy the dairy cow was standing in the yard after milking.

"Morning Daisy," said Farmer John. "You're putting on weight, aren't you?"

"Mooo!" said Daisy. "Rubbish. I'm just big boned."

"Oh," said Farmer John. "Is that it? I don't know though...I think you need to slim down a bit. From now on you'll just have hay and water until you get thinner."

Daisy was a bit alarmed. "Hay and water! But how am I supposed to live on that?" she said.

"You'll survive," said Farmer John. "If I have to go on a diet, so do you!" And he pushed off to see the pigs.

Suzie the sow was scratching herself on the pig-pen wall.

"Morning, Suzie," said Farmer John. "You're looking a bit porky. I think I've been feeding you too much. From now on you'll only get half a bucket of barley and no milk."

"What!" Suzie cried. "You can't be serious!"

"If you want to lose weight," said Farmer John, "you have to make sacrifices."

"But I don't want to lose weight," said Suzie. "I'm quite happy the way I am."

"You may be, but I'm not," said Farmer John. "It's not just you -Daisy is dieting too - so you're in good company." And he marched off to see the sheep.

Mavis the ewe was nibbling some hay when Farmer John arrived.

"Morning Mavis," said Farmer John. "You *do* look big - but I can do something about that!"

"What do you mean?" said Mavis.

"It's time you lost some weight," said Farmer John. "I'm doing it, and so is Daisy and Suzie. We'll all diet together."

"Oh dear," said Mavis. "But I like my food!"

"Well," said Farmer John, "you'll have to eat less from now on...it'll be healthier for you, and cost me less too."

Mavis looked very fed up. "What a pain!" she thought. "I have a healthy appetite. I'll have to see about this."

Farmer John went back to the house for lunch. Wendy was doing something with a lettuce in the kitchen. "Lettuce!" said Farmer John. "That's rabbit food. You're surely not going to give me lettuce for lunch?"

"Lettuce is very good for you," said Wendy, "and it isn't fattening either. Now just sit down, and eat what I give you."

Farmer John tucked into his salad. It was very crunchy, but not very filling. When he had finished he rubbed his hands together.

"Now what about one of those nice apple pies," he said. "You know how much I love them."

Wendy shook her head. "No puddings for you from now on," she said. "Have an apple, instead."

Farmer John munched his apple in silence; he was beginning to regret this dieting business!

When Farmer John went to bed that night he was feeling very hungry. His stomach growled and growled and he couldn't get off to sleep. Finally, in the middle of the night he carefully slipped out of bed, and crept downstairs.

He went into the kitchen and opened the fridge. There was a delicious looking steak and kidney pudding staring at him from the shelf. "Mmm!" Farmer John smacked his lips. "That looks nice," he said, and began to stuff it into his mouth. Dribbles of gravy ran down his chin, and it wasn't long before he had finished the whole lot.

He rubbed his tummy. "That's better," he said, and looked in the fridge again. A portion of apple pie and cream sat in a dish. He fetched a spoon and had soon gobbled it all up. He was feeling really full. He crept back upstairs again and crawled into bed, and was soon sound asleep.

Mavis the ewe couldn't sleep either. Her tummy was rumbling. She got up. "This is no good," she said, and trotted off. She went across the yard to the feed store, and opened the door. She crept inside. She thought she was alone but when she turned on the light Suzie and Daisy were there, munching away on a bag of barley.

Daisy and Suzie looked very guilty. They let out a sigh of relief. "Oh it's you, Mavis. We thought it was Farmer John. Come and join us."

Mavis joined in at the feed bag. "This barley's good," said Mavis. "I haven't eaten a thing all day."

"Nor have we," said Suzie and Daisy. "It's not fair - just because Farmer John's on a diet doesn't mean *we* have to go on one too. Do you know what we've just seen? We were passing the farmhouse and the kitchen light was on...and we saw Farmer John at the fridge with his face full of apple pie!"

"What a rotten cheat!" said Mavis. "We'll have to do something about this..."

So the next night, when everyone had gone to sleep, the animals hid outside the kitchen door. At two o'clock someone came tiptoeing into the kitchen, and opened the fridge. The light shone on Farmer John's face, but just as he had started to tuck into a large tub of ice cream Daisy, Suzie and Mavis came rushing in and turned on the light. "GOTCHA!" they cried. Farmer John jumped a mile in the air and dropped the ice cream on the floor. His face was covered in Raspberry Ripple!

Wendy woke up, and dashed down the stairs. "What on earth is going on?" she said. Then she saw Farmer John's ice cream-covered face.

"JOHN STUBBLEFIELD!" she cried. "You naughty man - and I thought you were sticking to your diet. It looks more like you've got ice cream sticking to you. What a cheat!"

Farmer John looked very guilty. "I'm sorry," he said, "but I was *so* hungry."

All the animals laughed. "Don't worry, John, we've been doing the same thing too. That barley in the feed store is delicious!" Farmer John burst out laughing. "Well," he said, "it looks like we've all failed."

Wendy shook her head. "Not necessarily," she said, and she held out a coloured magazine with a picture of a man doing exercises, with the words "Lose weight and feel great" underneath. "You don't have to eat less to lose weight," she said. "You could just exercise more."

"What a good idea!" everyone said.

So the next day, Farmer John and his animals began exercising. Daisy was given a skipping rope. Mavis pedalled on an exercise bike and Suzie went jogging round the farm. Farmer John did fifty press ups in his bedroom every morning before breakfast.

It wasn't long before they began to lose weight and get in shape, and when they all weighed themselves they had lost stones. Wendy was very pleased with Farmer John.

"Well done," she said. "I think you deserve a fried breakfast now, considering all the effort you've put in."

Farmer John smiled. "Perhaps I won't have quite so much though - just two rashers of bacon, and one egg. I don't want to spoil all that hard work," he said.

Farmer John doesn't eat quite so much as he used to but when he feels peckish in the night he still comes down and raids the larder; because although he doesn't want to be *too* plump, he doesn't want to be too slim either!

FARMER JOHN'S LAZY DAY

Farmer John decides to take a day off...but he finds it difficult to cope with all the housework!

One sunny morning, Farmer John woke up and stretched. He yawned and opened his eyes.

"I'm getting too old for this farming lark," he said to Wendy, his wife. "I think I'll have a day off - you can do everything today, my dear."

"WHAT!" said Wendy. "But I've got all the housework to do."

"Well I'm sure you'll manage, dear," said Farmer John. "Now, what about a spot of breakfast in bed?"

"You'll be lucky!" said Wendy. "If I'm going to be dealing with farm work all day, I won't have time to cook you meals."

"But can't you be bothered to look after your husband?" said Farmer John.

"JOHN STUBBLEFIELD, you ungrateful man - look at everything I do for you…!"

Farmer John was a bit alarmed. "Don't worry, my dear," he said. "I'm sure you'll manage. You only have to milk and feed the cows, feed the sheep and the pigs, muck them out, collect the eggs, mow some grass and milk the cows again in the evening. I'm sure you can manage that."

"Well, if I do all that," said Wendy, "you'll have to do all the housework, and I'll expect you to cook me my meals as well."

"Oh dear," said Farmer John. "I was hoping to have a lazy day today. Oh well...it can't be all that difficult." And he turned over and started snoring. "Zzzzzzzz..."

Wendy was a bit fed up. "I'd better get out and milk those cows," she said, and climbed out of bed and struggled into her clothes. She wrestled her boots on, and went out into the yard. Daisy was standing by the water trough.

"Mooo!" she said. "Where's Farmer John this morning?"

"He's having a day off," said Wendy, "so I'm doing all the work instead."

"Mooo," said Daisy. "What a lazy farmer!"

"I don't think he's going to have such an easy day as he thinks," said Wendy. "He's got all the housework to do!"

"I bet he messes that up," said Daisy. "I don't think Farmer John is very house-trained, you know."

"Hmmm," said Wendy. "Perhaps you're right - oh well, we'll see!"

Farmer John was still in bed when Wendy came in for breakfast. "Come on John," she said, "where's my breakfast? I'm starving! Can't you be bothered to look after your wife?"

Farmer John clambered out of bed. He pulled his clothes on and rushed downstairs in a panic. He tossed some eggs into a pan with some bacon, and began frying. He turned the eggs and bacon out onto a plate, and handed it to Wendy.

"What's this?" said Wendy.

"Bacon and eggs," said Farmer John.

"But the yolks are all broken," said Wendy. "It's more like an omelette!"

"I'm sorry," said Farmer John, "but I was in a hurry."

"Oh well," said Wendy, "I suppose I'd better eat it - but I'll expect you to do better at lunchtime." And she gobbled down her food and went out.

At the sheep shed, Mavis was chewing some hay when Wendy arrived. "Baa," she said, "where's Farmer John?"

"I'm doing all the work today, Mavis," said Wendy. "Farmer John is having a lazy day. He's only got the housework to do...he can't make much of a mess of that!"

Mavis tutted. "I'm not so sure," she said. "He makes quite a mess of the farm-work sometimes!"

In the house, Farmer John was trying to get to grips with the vacuum cleaner.

"How do you turn it on?" he wondered. He tried pressing a switch, but the machine just bent double. He pressed another switch and the machine began to blow dust everywhere.

"OH NO!" Farmer John cried. "It's supposed to suck, not blow."

He tried another switch and the machine began to make crunching and grinding noises. He looked down. It was trying to eat up the rug, and had wound it up round its beaters.

"Blast!" said Farmer John. "What do I do now? This machine has a mind of its own."

He switched the machine off and unwound the carpet from the beaters, and stood it up straight.

"I'd better get a dustpan and brush for all this dust," he said. He got down on his hands and knees and brushed up as much of the dust as he could, and emptied it into the bin.

"Perhaps the bag is full," he thought, and opened up the machine. He took out the dust bag but he got it upside down, and dust went everywhere again.

"Rats!" thought Farmer John. "This housework is a bit more difficult than I thought."

Eventually he got things tidied up, and decided to vacuum the stairs. He uncoiled the hose from the vacuum cleaner and put it together. He was left with a spare end.

"Now, where does this go?" he wondered. Finally he put it all together and began on the stairs, but he got tangled up with the flex and the hose, and Farmer John and the machine fell all the way down the stairs to the bottom.

"OUCH, OUCH, OUCH!" Poor Farmer John was rather bruised by his experiences.

"I think I'll leave the vacuuming for now," he said. "There must be other easier things I can do!"

Wendy was outside, feeding the pigs. Suzie the sow was scratching herself on the pig-pen wall when Wendy arrived. "Where's Farmer John?" she asked.

"He's supposed to be having a lazy day," said Wendy, "but I don't think he realizes that housework is quite hard to do."

Suzie grunted. "Huh," she said, "that sounds about right! I reckon that Farmer John will be very keen to do the farm-work tomorrow...you mark my words!"

Wendy laughed. "I bet you're right," she said, and went back to the house for lunch.

Farmer John was banging around in the kitchen. Wendy looked at the state of the carpets.

"Where's all this dust come from?" she asked. "I thought you were supposed to do the cleaning?"

"I did," said Farmer John from the kitchen, "but your machine's hopeless. It won't do what it's told."

Wendy was a bit cross. "Now I'll have twice as much to do tomorrow!" she complained. "Now, where's my lunch?"

Farmer John put a plate down in front of her.

"What's this?" said Wendy.

"It's one of my specials," said Farmer John, "Meatballs and gravy."

"But it's out of a tin," said Wendy.

"Well," said Farmer John, "it's all I could do in the time."

"I can't eat this," said Wendy, "you've burnt the gravy! I think I'll just make myself a sandwich."

Poor Farmer John; he wasn't having a very good time of it! Wendy went out.

"This is no good," said Farmer John to himself. "I'm supposed to be having a lazy day - but I'd better do the washing, or I'll never hear the last of it!" He put all the clothes in the washing machine and shut the door.

"This can't be very difficult," he said as he set the dial to 'Hot Wash'. "Now perhaps I can have a break," he thought, but then he realized he hadn't washed up from lunch. He had to scour the pots and pans that he'd burnt and it wasn't long before the washing was ready. He took the clothes out. The woolly jumpers had shrunk and the white clothes had all turned pink! He'd washed them with his red socks.

"Oh bother!" said Farmer John. "Oh well," and he put the clothes in the dryer. "I'd better do some dusting," he said.

He got a dust cloth and started polishing the ornaments on the mantle-piece. A piece of china slipped out of his hands and landed - "CRASH!" - on the floor. It was broken to smithereens.

"Oh blast," said Farmer John, "now I'm for it! That was Wendy's favourite ornament. I'd better not do any more dusting."

He went to the dryer and removed the clothes. "Perhaps I can do some ironing," he thought.

He got hold of the ironing board and tried to set it up. It was a bit like a deck chair, and he ended up with the board upside down. Then he trapped his fingers as he set it up the right way round.

"OUCH!" he cried. "It's bitten me!" Eventually he found the iron and set the dial to 'Hot'. He got a shirt and started ironing, but the steam iron started leaking water all over it.

"Oh bother," he said.

He was in the middle of ironing his shirt when the telephone rang. He left the iron and answered the phone. When he got back, he'd burnt an iron shaped hole in the back of his shirt.

"Oh blow!" cried Farmer John. "I can't do anything right!"

Just then, Wendy came in for some tea. She was not best pleased when she saw what Farmer John had done.

"JOHN STUBBLEFIELD," she cried, "you ham-fisted man, what *have* you been up to? I think we'd better stop right now. I'll cook dinner, and you can milk the cows."

Farmer John was a bit relieved. "I don't think I'm cut out for housework, my dear," he said. "You do it much better than me."

"Yes," said Wendy. "No more lazy days for you. I can't trust you to do anything in the house - it's outside for you from now on!"

"Phew," said Farmer John. "Thank goodness for that!" And he gave Wendy a huge hug.

FARMER JOHN'S GREAT EGGS-CAPADE

Farmer John's hens aren't laying very well - but it isn't long before he has more eggs than he knows what to do with!

It was morning on Thistledown Farm and Farmer John was up and about, collecting eggs from his chickens. He counted them as he carefully put them in his bucket. "One, two, three, four," he said to himself, "five, six, seven, eight. Hmm, that's not very many...my hens usually lay more than this. I wonder what's wrong?"

He carried the eggs back to the house, took off his boots, and went into the kitchen. Wendy, his wife, was doing some baking. "I don't know what's happened to my hens," he said. "They don't seem to have been laying many eggs recently. I wonder what could be the matter with them?"

"Perhaps they've had a fright," said Wendy. "You never know - Charlie the fox may be around."

"Oh dear," said Farmer John. "Do you think so?"

"It's possible," said Wendy. "You could talk to them and find out."

"That's a good idea," said Farmer John. "I'll ask Hilda. She's my best layer - she always knows what's going on." And he toddled off back up to the hen house.

He found Hilda the hen giving herself a dust bath in the chicken run. "Morning, Hilda!" said Farmer John. "Can you give me a minute?"

"Of course," clucked Hilda. "What's up, John?"

"Well," said Farmer John, "you don't seem to have been laying many eggs lately. Has anything happened to upset you?"

Hilda looked puzzled. "I don't think so," she said. "Perhaps if you gave us a bit more corn? We might lay more eggs if you did that."

"Do you really think so?" said Farmer John.

"Oh yes," said Hilda. "I'm sure we would - you'd have eggs coming out of your ears if you fed us more!"

"Good-oh," said Farmer John. "I'll start right now." He went and got a bag of chicken feed, and filled the birds' feeder right up to the top. "There," he said chuckling to himself, "now we'll see how many eggs we get tomorrow."

That night, he went to bed and dreamed about his chickens. He dreamt that his birds laid dozens and dozens and dozens of eggs and that he was covered in a pile of eggs that he didn't know what to do with. He dreamt that he was rolling around in eggs and that he was covered in egg yolk, and he cried out in his sleep, "Help, HELP!" Wendy had to shake him awake and he told her his dream. Wendy told him to calm down and not to be so silly. Eventually, when he woke up the next morning, he was exhausted. He had large bags under his eyes and his hair was a mess.

He couldn't wait for his breakfast. He dashed out of the house and ran up to the chicken shed and opened the door. All his birds were perched right at the top of the shed on top of piles and piles of eggs!

"Oh good heavens," said Farmer John. "My nightmare has come true! What on earth am I going to do with all this lot?" Hilda laughed. "I told you you'd have eggs coming out of your ears," she said. "You'll need more than a bucket to collect all these."

Farmer John scratched his head. He frowned; then he had an idea. "I know! I'll ask Brian my neighbour to help," he said. "He'll know what to do." It wasn't long before

Brian was helping him collect all the eggs from the hen house, and putting them safely in the barn on the straw.

"What you need is a machine," said Brian, "to sort them out into different sizes and put them in boxes to sell." Farmer John found an egg sorter for sale in the paper and soon had it delivered. It was a very strange contraption with lots of belts and pulleys and dials and lights, and when they switched it on it made a loud chattering noise. They put the eggs in one end and they came out the other in different sizes - small, medium and large, ready to put into boxes.

Farmer John was very pleased, but just as he thought he had everything under control, his machine began to make crunching and grating noises. Then all hell was let loose. Eggs went flying everywhere. Farmer John standing at one end had a dozen eggs drop onto his head, and he got covered in sticky egg yolk!

"HO HO HO!" Brian laughed and laughed at him, and Farmer John didn't look very pleased, but Brian soon stopped laughing...Farmer John had picked up an egg and lobbed it at him. SPLAT! The egg broke on his head, and Brian found himself with egg on his face!

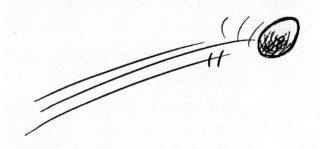

"GRRR!" He was a bit angry, and started chucking eggs back at Farmer John. Soon Farmer John and Brian were having a serious egg fight, and the machine was joining in. Wendy heard the commotion and came running.

"What on earth is going on!" she cried. "JOHN STUBBLEFIELD, what *are* you doing now!" But she didn't escape for very long. An egg came sailing through the air and landed - CRUNCH! - all over her hair, and dribbled down her face. Wendy looked very cross. She picked up some stray eggs and chucked them at Farmer John, and Brian did the same!

Poor Farmer John...his dream really had come true! He was plastered in egg from head to foot. There was egg everywhere - everyone was covered - but eventually the machine ran out of eggs, and came to a standstill. Brian, Wendy and Farmer John stopped and looked at themselves. They all burst out laughing. There weren't any eggs left for them to throw.

"It looks like the yolk's on us," said Farmer John. Wendy and Brian groaned.

"We need a bath," said Wendy.

"What's for dinner?" asked Farmer John.

"What about an omelette?" said Wendy.

"Oh no," said Farmer John. "I don't think I could face another egg today."

"I agree," said Wendy. "I think eight eggs a day is quite enough for anybody."

"Eggs-actly," said Brian.

"Eggs-tremely," said Farmer John.

"Eggs-traordinary!" said Wendy - and they all set about cleaning up the mess!

FARMER JOHN'S TIME MACHINE

Farmer John is having a bad day...so he decides to go back in time to put everything right!

One fine Tuesday morning Farmer John jumped out of bed, dressed in a hurry and dashed out to milk the cows. He was late and he rushed through the milking.

"Moo," said Daisy. "Steady on, John - it's not a race, you know!"

Farmer John panted, "I know, Daisy, but I've got to get on - the tanker will be here soon to pick up the milk. If I'm not finished by the time he gets here he'll leave without it."

He was halfway through when he heard the milk lorry come down the lane. "Oh dear!" he flustered. "I'm not finished yet. I hope he'll wait." But the driver was in a hurry.

"I'm sorry, John," he said. "If you're not finished, the milk won't be cool enough. I'll have to miss you out this morning." He drove off.

Farmer John was a bit annoyed with himself. "Silly me," he said. "If I hadn't overslept I wouldn't have missed the tanker. Oh well, I haven't got room in the tank for two days milk...I'll have to throw this lot away." He pulled the plug and the milk gushed out.

Daisy mooed, "Look at all that lovely milk - what a waste!"

"I know," said Farmer John, "but there's nothing I can do, I'm afraid."

He stomped back to the farmhouse. He was in a bad mood. "Where's my breakfast?" he said to Wendy his wife. "I'm starving."

"You're late," said Wendy. "I haven't got time to cook it - I'm off to work in a minute."

"But I've just done all the milking!" said Farmer John. "Can't you be bothered to look after your husband?"

Wendy looked at him. "JOHN STUBBLEFIELD," she fumed, "you ungrateful man! Look at everything I do for you. I cook and clean and look after the children and do the books and feed the calves, and on top of that I have a job to do. You're the most ungrateful man I know!" And she went out and slammed the door.

"Oh dear," thought Farmer John. "I've upset her...what am I going to do now?"

He made his breakfast, and munched it in silence. There was a knock at the door. Pete the postman was there with a parcel. "Morning, John!" he said. "Lovely day, isn't it?"

Farmer John scowled. "Nice for you, maybe," he said. "All you have to do is deliver letters - what an easy life!" Pete was taken aback. "All you do is swan around in that red van of yours chatting to people all day. Why don't you get a proper job?" And Farmer John slammed the door.

Pete was a bit upset. "Why's he so angry at me?" he wondered. "He'll be lucky to get his letters tomorrow!" He drove off in a huff.

Farmer John lay on the sofa and went to sleep. He was woken by a knock at the door. It was old Mrs. Dingle from down the road. "John," she puffed, "I'm sorry to bother you, but your pigs have got out - they're in my garden."

"WHAT!" cried Farmer John. "Oh bother...can't you do something about it? I'm having a bad day."

"But John," said Mrs. Dingle, "they're eating my petunias!"

"I'll come when I'm ready," said Farmer John, and shut the door.

It was the middle of the afternoon when he woke up. He climbed off the settee, and stretched. "I must collect the eggs," he thought, and he toddled out to the chicken house.

He got a tray and began collecting all the eggs. The hens were outside pecking around in the chicken run. He had collected two dozen eggs and was walking back to the house when he tripped over a tree root in the ground. The eggs went sailing through the air and landed – SPLAT! - in the yard. "BOTHER!" cried Farmer John. "They're all broken - another waste! I'm staying indoors today...nothing's going right! If I go outside again, something bad is bound to happen."

It was evening when Wendy came back from work. She came into the house and started banging around in the kitchen. She didn't talk to Farmer John; she was still angry with him. Farmer John began to feel a bit ashamed of himself. "Oh dear," he thought, "I *have* been a bit grumpy today...and oh my goodness, my sheep need some more hay. Oh well, it's too late now - they'll be OK till morning."

He sat and watched the telly. It was Dr. Who. Dr. Who was able to travel backwards and forwards in time in a time machine. Farmer John had an idea. "What if I could go back in time?" he said. "Then I could start the day again, and everything would be all right." He leapt out of his chair and went out to his workshop, and closed the door.

Strange banging and crashing noises could be heard, a tapping and sawing noise, and then a bright light from the welder. Soon the workshop doors opened and a strange looking machine appeared, pushed by Farmer John. He stood it in the yard and climbed inside. He pulled a lever and a lot of very bright lights started to flash on and off. Suddenly the machine started to disappear, and soon it wasn't there at all.

Farmer John looked at the levers in front of him. One said 'Backwards' and another said 'Forwards'. He set the distance to one day, closed his eyes, and pulled the lever. He was rushing through a dark tunnel - and before he could say "Jack Robinson", he was back in the farmyard at the break of day. He went into the farmhouse and looked at the calendar. It said Wednesday.

"But yesterday was Monday," thought Farmer John. "Oh no, I must have pulled the wrong lever - I've gone forward a day instead of back! Oh well, let's see what happens tomorrow...it might be interesting."

Wendy spotted him. "Oh John," she said, "thank you ever so much for those flowers - it was so thoughtful of you. I'm sorry about yesterday."

Farmer John was a little taken aback. "But I didn't give you any flowers," he said.

"Yes you did," said Wendy. "You went out and picked some freesias from the garden late last night, and put them on my dressing table. I found them this morning. Do you want me to cook your breakfast, my dear?"

"Yes. Thanks," said Farmer John; he was a little surprised.

"Oh, by the way," said Wendy, "it was a good job you dropped those eggs yesterday - they were all rotten."

"Really?" said Farmer John. "Goodness - that was a stroke of luck."

Just then, there was a knock at the door. It was Pete the postman with the letters. "Morning, John!" he said cheerfully. "Thanks for apologising on the telephone last night...it made my day. I thought it wasn't like you to be so rude."

"That's all right, Pete," said Farmer John, rather guiltily. "I'm sorry about what I said. I know being a postman is hard work really - I was just in a bit of a bad mood, that's all."

"Don't worry, John," said the postman. "I understand."

Farmer John finished his breakfast and walked down to the pig-pens. The pigs were back where they should be. "Oh John," they said. "We're sorry we ran off yesterday. We all came back because we didn't like being away from the farm."

Farmer John laughed. "That's good," he said, "but what about old Mrs. Dingle? She was very upset."

"She was pleased with us," said the pigs, "because we rooted around and turned over her vegetable patch. She'd been looking for someone to dig that for ages, but couldn't find anyone."

"Well," said Farmer John, "it seems like things have turned out quite nicely...but what about my sheep?"

He toddled off up to the sheep shed. The sheep were nibbling at some hay. "Morning John," they bleated. "What lovely hay, it's so sweet and delicious. It was a good thing we didn't get any last night - it has made us appreciate it more. You don't realise how nice a thing is if you get it all the time."

"That's true," said Farmer John, "but there's one thing that happened yesterday that hasn't turned out right. The milk...I had to throw it all away."

Just then, Mike the milkman drove into the yard on his milk float. "Hello," he said. "I'm from the dairy. We had a bad batch of milk yesterday and we had to throw it all away. I'm just here to tell you that you'll get paid for yesterday's milk just the same."

Farmer John beamed. "Thank you," he said, "what a nice surprise!"

He waved to the man, and climbed back into his time machine. "I'm going back to yesterday," he said. "It just goes to show that you don't need to go back in time to put everything right, because everything turns out for the best anyway." He pulled the lever. The lights started to flash and very soon he was back on Thistledown Farm on Tuesday evening.

"Now, let's go out and pick those flowers," he said and he put on his boots and went out into the garden...

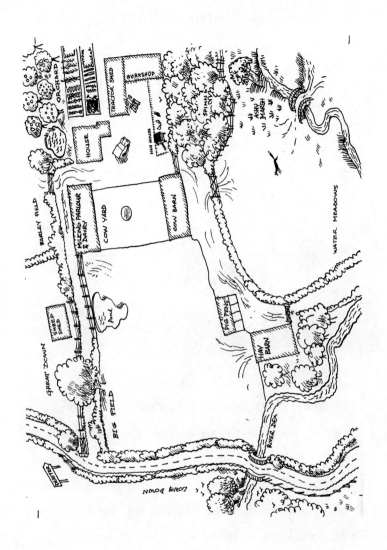

151

ABOUT THE AUTHOR

David Charles Evans BSc.(Hons) was born in Nakuru, Kenya into an old farming family, his grandparents being Kenya pioneers from Shropshire, and was brought up on the family farm in West Devon.

He studied agriculture at Seale-Hayne College, Newton Abbot and spent his time pedigree sheep breeding and sheep shearing before settling in Exeter and developing his ideas for a humorous children's character based upon the eccentricities of all the farmers he has known and Farmer John Stubblefield was born. David is currently an active member of Exeter Writers and has many more Farmer John stories up his sleeve.

Contact David at www.farmerjohnbooks.co.uk

ABOUT THE ILLUSTRATOR

Jake Tebbit has been an illustrator for all his working life.

He trained as a graphic designer at Kingston School of Art and worked first as a background artist at Halas & Batchelor, the British Animation Company, then moved on to become Senior Editorial Artist for Reed Publishing, before going Freelance in 1977.

He has worked with many publishers of Children's story books, Educational text books, Agricultural and reference books and his pictures have been used to illustrate several of the BBC's *Jackanory* programmes.

In his spare time he teaches Illustration to students at a local Sixth Form College and is well known for his 'jolly' cartoons, which can be viewed on his website:

www.jaketebbit.co.uk